TEKNON
AND THE
CHAMPION
WARRIORS

A SON'S QUEST
FOR COURAGEOUS MANHOOD

BY BRENT SAPP

ILLUSTRATED BY SERGIO CARIELLO

FAMILYLIFE™
Bringing Timeless Principles Home

Little Rock, Arkansas

Teknon and the CHAMPION Warriors

Published by FamilyLife, a division of Campus Crusade for Christ.

Author: Brent Sapp
Senior Editor: Ben Colter
Editorial Team: Rick Blanchette, Stephen W. Sorenson,
                 Anne Wooten, and Fran Taylor

Illustrator: Sergio Cariello
Designer: Jerry McCall

Printed in the United States of America.
ISBN 1-57229-219-9

NOTE: This book is intended for boys ages 11 to 16. It contains some mature subject matter addressing dating, sexual temptation, and pornography.

Bringing Timeless Principles Home
Dennis Rainey, Executive Director
3900 N. Rodney Parham Road
Little Rock, AR 72212
(501) 223-8663
1-800-FL-TODAY
www.familylife.com
A division of Campus Crusade for Christ

Dedicated to
Mom and Dad

A pair of champions

Teknon
and the
Champion
Warriors

Contents

COURAGE · HONOR · ATTITUDE · MENTAL TOUGHNESS · PURITY · INTEGRITY · OWNERSHIP · NAVIGATION

THE
CHAMPION
WARRIOR CREED

"IF I HAVE THE COURAGE TO FACE MY FEARS; HONOR, WHICH I SHOW TO PNEUMA+ AND MY FELLOW MAN; THE PROPER ATTITUDE CONCERNING MYSELF AND MY CIRCUMSTANCES; THE MENTAL TOUGHNESS REQUIRED TO MAKE HARD DECISIONS; PURITY OF HEART, MIND, AND BODY; THE INTEGRITY TO STAND FOR WHAT I BELIEVE, EVEN IN THE MOST DIFFICULT SITUATIONS; EFFECTIVE OWNERSHIP OF ALL THAT IS ENTRUSTED TO ME; AND FOCUSED NAVIGATION IN ORDER TO SUCCESSFULLY CHART MY COURSE IN LIFE; I WILL LIVE AS A TRUE CHAMPION WARRIOR, COMMITTED TO BATTLING EVIL, AND CHANGING MY WORLD FOR PNEUMA'S GLORY."

* Note: The character Pneuma represents God in this fictional story.

The Cast of Characters

Teknon

Kratos

Epios (Epps)

Artios (Arti)

Tharreo (Tor)

Mataios (Matty)

Phileo (Phil)

Magos

Scandalon

Footsoldier

Rhegma

Leviathan

Seismos

Pseudes

Amacho

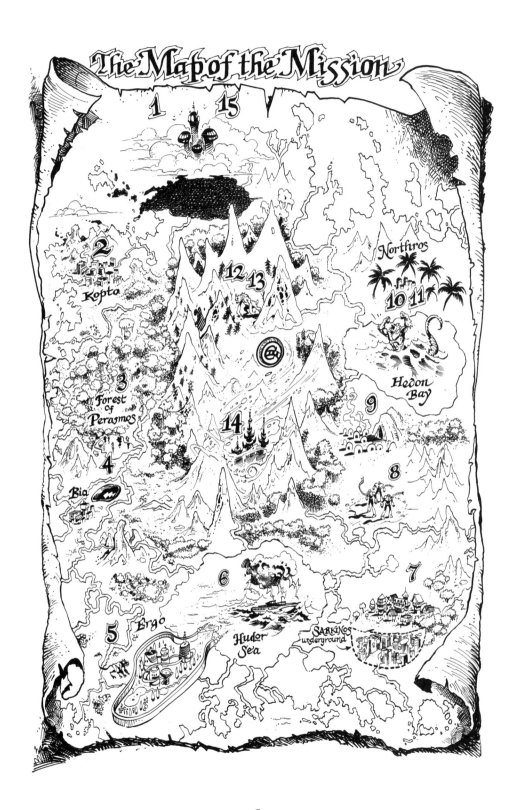

Destination: Kairos

Teknon narrowly dodged the horn of the charging hodgebeast. He jumped up, grabbed a vine, and nimbly swung up into a large tree. Perched on a limb, he spotted another vine and jumped toward it. He swung out over the river and dropped when he saw that the water was deep enough. A long-tailed gorgon surfaced and chased the boy to shore, nearly catching him in its massive jaws.

Teknon left the water and ran across a field of high brush as small explosions burst around him. He chose his steps carefully so as not to trigger hidden detonators. As he left the field, several creatures with bulging eyes and multiple arms emerged from the brush carrying weapons. The creatures threw energy bolts at him that he dodged with ease as they pursued him through the jungle. Suddenly, Teknon spotted a cliff ahead with a hundred meter drop into a river below. The creatures closed in, and Teknon prepared to leap.

At that moment, a set of doors appeared in Teknon's path, sliding open into a large room. Teknon entered through the doors, which closed immediately behind him and right in

front of the trailing creatures. Teknon stopped and grabbed his chest, breathing heavily. He used his sleeve to wipe dirt and sweat from his brow as a lean, muscular man smiled and threw him a towel. Teknon caught the towel and held it to his face.

"I think we're babying you, Teknon," the man said. "How long do you expect us to keep the training simulator on level four?"

"Matty," Teknon said, still heaving, "what did you want me to do, tell the gorgon I'd go best two out of three with him?" They both laughed. "Believe me," Teknon said as he draped the towel around his neck and stepped into his father's office, "I'm pushing as hard as I can to get in shape for this trip."

Kratos' office was, without a doubt, Teknon's favorite room in the house. For most of his life, Teknon had lived in this tri-level mansion suspended almost 2000 meters above the surface of his home planet, Basileia. His father designed the spacious home that displayed many of the inventions he developed while working with the government. Now their home hovered silently in the sky, powered by three hydronic engines.

Teknon dropped into an overstuffed chair. His father stood slowly, still deeply concentrating on the maps and diagrams displayed on the large, flat screen embedded in the center table. Four men joined Kratos at the table as he stroked his bearded chin and motioned for his son to look. Teknon greeted Artios—whom the rest of the team called Arti—and Epios, known as Epps. Mataios—the jovial Matty—also greeted him with a firm grasp, and Tor— short for Tharreo—slapped the youth on his back so hard it made him stumble. As he walked toward his father, Teknon spotted a strange, circular object leaning against his father's gear.

"What's with the oversized dinner platter?" Teknon asked.

"It's called a Hoplon," Kratos responded.

Teknon picked up the handsome, metallic object. "Hoplon? Sounds like something a razorrabbit would do if you scared it." He looked at Kratos and smiled. "Seriously, what's it for? Is it an antique? I've only read about warriors using shields like this in the history files."

"I designed it. It's a new military project," Kratos said.

"You mean it's a weapon? How much did the military fork out this time?"

"Seven million dinar from the treasury. I put in the remaining five million."

"Twelve million dinar! For one shield?" Teknon held the shield with both hands at arm's length. He smirked. "You're kidding, right? Dad, it's only a shield. Why in the world did you help finance something like this?"

Kratos walked over to the picture window to get his cup of hot nela. He carefully took a sip from the steaming cup and looked out over the clouds and the beautiful mountainous terrain below. "I have my reasons. I wanted exclusive rights to this particular prototype. I'll design another after the military sees it and starts drooling."

"But what's it for, I mean beyond the obvious?" Teknon asked, puzzled. He looked at the shield, scanning its circular edge. "And what's this design on the front? I've never seen anything like it."

Kratos put his hand on Teknon's shoulder and looked over his back. "It's the mark of the ancient CHAMPION Warriors. It took me a while to find the image in the archives. There's quite a history behind that one. I thought it would be a proper symbol for the Hoplon."

"Okay," Teknon responded, "I'll bite. What kind of history?"

Kratos smiled and continued. "The CHAMPION Warriors were a courageous team of people that, several centuries ago, banded together to protect the citizens of Basileia from an evil army of aggressors called the Daimons. The Daimons threatened to overthrow and rule the planet. These CHAMPION Warriors gained respect and admiration because of their courage, their high code of character, and their strong faith in Pneuma, the Eternal Spirit."

Kratos put his cup on the table and crossed his arms. "These warriors were fierce defenders. Each of them carried a shield at all times. The shields were designed specifically to complement their defensive fighting style, called amuno. Each shield was engraved with this insignia. Through the years, the people of Basileia began to look for this symbol, which represented the heroes who defended them from enemy aggression. Basileians knew that if ever they fell under attack, the men who carried the CHAMPION Warrior shield would soon come to their aid."

"Sounds very noble," Teknon quipped. "So what does this expensive piece of hardware do, anyway?"

"I think I'll keep that to myself for the time being," Kratos responded.

"What? Aw, c'mon!" Teknon pleaded. "This isn't one of those 'If I told you, I'd have to feed you to the swampcrushers' kinds of things, is it?"

"Something like that," Kratos said. He glanced toward the other men. His friends nodded. "It will come in very handy as we head out on our mission."

"Okay, so what do you do with it when you're not using it?" Teknon said as he followed his father out of the room. "Where do you put it?"

Tharreo leaned over and put his hand on Teknon's shoulder. "He puts it over the yapper of mouthy young men. You know, kid, you could talk the ears off a statue." He laughed and pushed the boy away.

"I'm just curious, Tor," Teknon said to his grinning mentor.

Kratos walked into the training room. Teknon followed and watched his father open a custom-designed silver case. From it, Kratos pulled out what appeared to be a pair of shoulder pads without the padding.

"This is where I put the Hoplon," Kratos said in a low tone as he held up the harness and slipped his arms and head through the openings. Metallic straps crossed over his chest, with a medallion-shaped fixture shining in the middle of the straps. With the harness in place, he carefully held the Hoplon with both hands and placed it over his shoulders. To Teknon's amazement, when Kratos let go of the shield it immediately clamped to the shoulder harness. The harness and shield looked like one unit.

"Whooaaa!" Teknon said, surprised. "How did that happen?"

Kratos turned and faced Teknon. "The Hoplon and its harness are programmed for my particular brain waves. *I think* a command and it responds." Kratos shifted his shoulders. "When my body comes into contact with the Hoplon, it gives me ..." Kratos stopped himself. "Well, anyway, it won't work for anyone else. Pretty swift, eh, Son?"

"You could say that," Teknon responded, his eyes wide. While Teknon continued to gawk at his father's invention, his younger sister, Hilarotes, ran in and hugged her father.

"Good night, Dad," she said as she squeezed Kratos' neck. "Mom says you're leaving early in the morning and that I need to say good-bye now. I'm really going to miss you."

"Just me, Hilly?" Kratos said, still holding her in his arms. "Your brother's leaving, too, you know."

"I know," Hilly said in a whisper as she turned around and looked at Teknon. "But he won't miss me."

Kratos smiled. "Well, I'll sure miss you," he said with one last squeeze. Hilly grinned and said good-bye to the other men as she started out of the room. She stopped at the door and looked back at Teknon. He was sitting down and looking out of the window.

"Bye, Teknon," Hilly said. "Take care."

"Yep," Teknon said, not turning around.

His sister's mouth wrinkled as she looked at her father. Kratos nodded and threw her a kiss as she went off to bed.

Kratos took off the harness and put it back into the case. He stood up and stretched. "Well, gents, let's turn in. We've got quite a day ahead of us."

"The equipment is packed and ready," Artios said.

"See you at dawn's light," Tor added. He slapped Kratos on the back and walked into the next room. The other mentors followed.

A few minutes later, Teknon was on his way to bed. He paused as he passed by the slightly opened door of Tor's room, noticing that his hulking mentor was on his knees, his head bowed. Teknon heard Tor saying, " ... and I ask you once again, my Warrior King, for the strength and perseverance to carry out the mission that You have given us. I want Your will to be done—nothing more, nothing less, nothing else."

Teknon had seen Tor speak like this before, but he was still taken back by the sight of the mighty warrior, who towered above all other members of the team, humbling himself in such a manner. Teknon lingered a moment before continuing down the hall to his room.

That night Teknon dreamed about the journey ahead. Images of strange places flowed through his thoughts. He tossed as he saw himself in battle, fighting side by side with his father and mentors. Powerful, frightening creatures surrounded them on all sides. As they closed in, Teknon woke drenched in sweat. Light gleamed through his window. It was time. The day was finally here.

Teknon got dressed and shuffled to the table for breakfast. He joined the mentors as his mother entered from the kitchen carrying several steaming containers of food. His mouth watered as he sniffed the sumptuous pinplum soup and he filled his bowl to the brim. Teknon scooped the superb contents to his lips even before he settled into his chair, then he glanced across the table as Tor pushed an entire spice cake into his enormous mouth.

Kratos entered from his bedroom and walked across the room to his wife, Paideia. Teknon beamed as he saw his parents embrace.

"Teknon, is the show always this good in the morning?" Matty asked, nodding toward the boy's parents.

Teknon chuckled.

"All right," Tor said, wiping his mouth and standing. "Let's get this caravan in gear."

"You're sure he's ready for this, Kratos?" Paideia said as she went over to her son and put her hands on his shoulders.

"Don't worry, Mom," Teknon said. "I'll make sure Dad keeps his socks dry." His mother smiled. Teknon looked back one last time and picked up his pack.

"He's got to be ready, Paideia," Kratos said. "Too much is at stake. Don't worry, my love. I've got good company to help me." Kratos nodded in the direction of his friends. The four men walked over to the couple. One by one they hugged Paideia and walked outside toward the platform. Kratos embraced his wife again, kissed her gently, and turned to follow the men and his son.

"I know I'm leaving the business in capable hands," Kratos said, looking back. "You'll contact the clients about the synthetic spine contract?"

"Of course," Paideia responded. "I'll also put the finishing touches on the holographic helmet design. It will be ready for production when you get back."

"She'll probably double your profits by the time we return," Matty chuckled.

"I don't doubt it," Kratos said, smiling at his wife. "She's made our medical division what it is today."

"I'll be on my knees every day," Paideia said. "May Pneuma grant you wisdom and strength on your journey."

Kratos waved while all members of the team gathered on the particle assimilator. Artios stepped to the controls and began to set the coordinates for the planet Kairos. Kratos helped Teknon fasten his pack as they waited.

"Do you think I'm ready for this, Dad?" Teknon asked nervously.

"Matters most what *you* think," Kratos said, pulling the last strap on Teknon's pack.

"Magos will know we're coming, won't he?"

"Probably," Kratos replied.

"That means Scandalon and the others are already plotting a first attack with him," Teknon said, his voice quivering slightly.

"It's all right to be nervous," Kratos said. "The trick is learning to channel that nervous energy into something productive. You'll have plenty of opportunities to learn that on Kairos." Kratos grasped his son by the shoulders, turned him around, and looked him straight in the eye. "Remember, Teknon, we're all here to help you. You, Tor, Epps, Arti,

Matty, and I are all part of a team on this mission. Your mentors are brave and talented. And even one man with courage makes a majority. We'll be with you, no matter how crazy it gets. Don't forget that true warriors never let friends face danger alone."

Tor glanced at Artios. "You know we're pushing the limits of this contraption by trying to assimilate three lunar sections away."

Artios appeared unfazed by Tor's comment as he continued to adjust the assimilator and set the controls. "Next stop, Transfer Station 3, village of Kopto on the planet Kairos. Assimilation transfer in exactly 30 seconds."

"Just get us to the base, Arti," Matty joked, "plus or minus a solar system, if you don't mind."

"You know Arti doesn't understand plus or minus, Matty," Epios said. "He's always on target."

Arti grinned as he joined the other members of the team on the platform. All of them looked at each other with anticipation. Adrenaline coursed through Teknon's veins. They all faced forward while Kratos spoke the final words of initiation.

"My friends, no man is worthy who is not ready at all times to risk body, status, and life itself for a great cause. For His honor and glory!"

"For His honor and glory!" the rest echoed as they vanished from the platform.

The mission had begun.

MY ENEMY,
YOUR ENEMY

S ix individuals materialized on the raised platform. A
short, multi-antennaed operator manipulated the complex controls until Kratos and his team arrived at Transfer
Station 3 in Kopto.

Teknon was fascinated by the flurry of activity occurring
within the facility. Representatives from different tribes hus-
tled throughout the terminal, waiting for transport. Through
the large windows in front of the platform, Teknon could see
the entrance to the infamous Kopto Commercial Market,
where rows of shops and vendors lined the streets. Buyers
and sellers haggled over exotic items from almost every
mountain and coast in the system. His dad had previously
told Teknon of Kopto's reputation as a haven for the black
market and as a storehouse for stolen goods. Kratos raised
his hand slightly and motioned for his five companions to go
outside.

Once in the street, they chose a curbside restaurant where

they could sit down and survey the landscape. Matty waved for service.

"Not at all like the Kopto I remember," Tor growled. "Years ago this place was a calm lakeside village. People would come from all over the system to relax and shop here. Now look at it." He pointed to a group of vendors screaming and waving in each other's faces. "Smugglers and scratch-backs, the lot of 'em."

"Better keep one hand on your packs today, fellas," Kratos said, turning around slightly in his chair.

"Mind if I have a look around?" Teknon asked his father.

Kratos thought for a moment. "All right, but stay close. Conditions change quickly around here. Watch yourself, and your currency."

Teknon nodded as he got up from the table.

The market was especially busy at dusk as Teknon slowly pushed and bumped his way through the endless line of shops and booths. Fascinating oddities paraded before his eyes: unusual clothes, travel gear, and enticing technical gadgets. Teknon loved contraptions that were new and exciting. He walked from booth to booth, picking up items, examining them, all the while feeling the weight of the coins in his pocket. Finally, he saw an item he couldn't resist—a small, shiny object that fit snugly in the palm of his hand. The object had finger holes, which allowed it to fit securely in his grip. It looked like a weapon, and it glistened in the afternoon sun. The vendor saw Teknon's interest and said, "It's a Karionian Shocktech."

"What does it do?" Teknon asked.

"It shoots a stun beam from a distance of 25 meters," the vendor responded.

"Twenty-five meters?" Teknon responded, gripping the small gun and taking a simulated aim at a pole. "How much?"

"One hundred and thirty specas. Good price, yes?"

"One hundred and thirty?!" Teknon said, frowning as he felt the sealed pocket on his uniform that held his money. He carried one hundred and fifty specas that was supposed to last him the entire trip. Teknon ran his hand through his sandy blonde hair. *I don't have a weapon,* he thought. *If I were to buy this piece, Dad certainly wouldn't mind because I could be more prepared. It's not lethal. Nah, Dad wouldn't mind, would he? This thing has such a natural feel to it. I could carry it in my hand, or in my pocket. I really want this.* "One hundred," Teknon countered.

The vendor shrugged his shoulders, then reached for the weapon and took it from Teknon. "Sorry, my friend. I can see you're not quite ready for such a handsome and useful item. Perhaps in a few years when you're old enough. Come back then."

Teknon fumed. His eyebrows narrowed, and his forehead wrinkled. "Old enough?! One hundred and ten specas!"

"Thank you for your time, young sir," replied the vendor. "Now please, step aside for a paying customer."

"All right, all right, one hundred and thirty it is." Teknon grudgingly handed the peddler his currency. He didn't feel great about what he was doing, but he really wanted the Shocktech.

"You've made a wise choice," said the vendor, handing Teknon the weapon. "Remember, all sales are final."

Teknon barely heard the peddler's last words as he looked at the weapon in his hand. *This is going to be great,* he thought, as he went back to the cafe and rejoined his companions.

"Where did you go, Teknon?" his father asked. Teknon held his hand open to Kratos, revealing his new purchase. Kratos looked at the small weapon, then directly at Teknon, with eyebrows creased. "A Shocktech, right? How much did you pay?"

"One hundred and thirty specas," Teknon said. The youth glanced at Matty, who was grinning while nudging Arti in the ribs.

"We'll talk later about this," his father replied, obviously disappointed.

"So what's the plan, Kratos?" Epps asked.

"We want to make the forest by nightfall," Kratos responded. "From now on, no more assimilations."

"What?" Teknon said. "You mean we're going to walk?"

"Or find whatever other transportation is available," Tor responded as he poked Teknon slightly. "Ready for a little exercise?"

Kratos explained, "We can't use the assimilators, Teknon, because our molecular matrix will point a trail right to us. Magos could track us from station to station if we transferred." Kratos hesitated for a moment. "I wouldn't be surprised if we'd been noticed already."

"There they are!" a peddler standing nearby screamed as he pointed to Kratos. "Those are the scratchbacks who stole my week's earnings. They're the ones responsible for all of the thefts in the market."

Kratos looked up quickly, then gave Arti a nod. Arti, in turn, nodded to Tor, Matty, and Epps.

"Quickly, seize them before they get away!" shrieked the peddler. The vendors, first taken back by the loud accusation, began moving toward Kratos and his team.

Teknon felt his dad's hand on his arm, and the touch settled him. He watched curiously as his mentors prepared for action. Tor pushed up his sleeves to reveal two highly technical braces covering his limbs from wrist to elbow. Arti reached into his pack and produced a small face band, which he slid into position around the contour of his jaw and forehead. The round fixture in the middle of the face band began to glow. Epps jammed his hands into his pockets and pulled them out covered by metallic gloves, which were expanding in waves up his forearms. Teknon had never seen these devices before.

The vengeful peddler led the crowd, now only a few meters away. Kratos jumped to his feet. The other five immediately followed. A bright yellow beam shot from the center of Arti's face band, surrounding and immobilizing the entire mob. Only the ranting merchant, who started the riot, escaped the beam. Realizing his attack had lost its momentum, the stranger darted off to the side, down a deserted alley, and out of sight.

Teknon stood in silent amazement as he watched the entire mob frozen in its tracks by Arti's beam. Kratos

grabbed Teknon by the arm and barked at the other four, "Plan C-3! I've got Teknon. We'll meet you at the designated position. Good luck!" Kratos hurriedly pulled his son down the street.

"Later, my friends," Epps said, heading in another direction.

"Stay strong, and keep your wits about you, Epps," Tor yelled back as he took off.

"Have fun, gents," Matty said, squeezing Arti's shoulder from behind. He then raced off into the distance.

Arti, still focused on the crowd, released the beam. The would-be assailants fell limp to their knees, lightheaded and disoriented. With a subtle look of satisfaction, Arti silently slipped away.

Kratos and Teknon were running down an alley when they came to a massive stone wall with a thick metal door leading to the other side. Kratos scanned the wall quickly while Teknon tried to open the door.

"It's locked," Teknon said. He could hear a few merchants yelling to each other, obviously searching for the team.

"Stand back," Kratos ordered. Teknon stepped back and watched as the medallion on his father's harness began to glow. Kratos lunged forward and slammed his forearm into the door. Teknon heard mortar crack and his mouth dropped open as he saw the door rip from its hinges and crash to the ground.

Teknon felt his father's firm grip leading him through the doorway. Again they ran. Teknon tried to speak, but his father motioned to remain quiet as they passed through several other inhabited sections of the city. In less than an hour, they found themselves at the outskirts of Kopto.

Teknon, his eyes still glazed in bewilderment, asked "What happened back there?"

"Let's wait until we get to the edge of the Perasmos forest," Kratos said. "We'll find a place to make camp and then we'll talk."

Half an hour later, they found an excellent campsite. Kratos pulled a small, cylindrical illuminator from his pocket, gave it to Teknon, and pointed to a large rock a few meters away.

"Set it over there," Kratos said. "It will be dark soon." Teknon positioned the illuminator and twisted the top half of the container. Light immediately shone around the camp in a perfect square that covered 15,000 cubic meters. Kratos removed the Hoplon and harness, and then placed them on the ground at the edge of the light containment field. As he pressed the medallion on the harness, the shield tilted slightly into position. Kratos then rotated the medallion, and the shield began to sway back and forth in a circular motion.

"What's it doing, Dad?" Teknon asked.

"I've got it set on continuous scan," Kratos responded. "It will alert us if anyone comes within a thousand meters."

Father and son quickly ate a small but filling dehydrated dinner. Then they unfolded their bed pads. Teknon slowly stretched out on the thin cushion. It felt good to be off his feet.

"Anytime you're ready," Teknon said, folding his hands behind his head. His father smiled.

"You're probably a little curious about some of the things that happened today." Kratos said as he turned off the illuminator. He lay down on his pad and stared up at the sky.

"You got that right!" Teknon responded.

"Where should I start?"

"Well, for starters, what happened at the table? Who was the screamer, and what did he want with us?"

"He identified us as a band of scratchback thieves," Kratos said.

"Why us?" Teknon exclaimed. "Do we look like we just got off the freight ship from Rhaima? Why were we singled out, and how did we get out of there? What were those things on Tor's arms? And on Epp's hands? And what about Arti?"

"Slow down," Kratos replied. "For starters, I think the little riot-starter was Scandalon."

"Scandalon?" Teknon asked. "But why didn't we recognize him?"

"Remember," Kratos reminded, "Magos created Scandalon with the ability to assume any shape at any time. Scandalon's body is made up of millions of cooperative, miniature machines that can move independently yet link up with other surrounding machines. That's why his appearance can shift and change. Scandalon's purpose is to deceive, seduce, and incite violence. In this case, he created a lynch mob. Scandalon is the second most dangerous android that Magos controls."

"So he spotted us at the transfer station?" Teknon asked.

"Scandalon was probably one of many of Magos' henchmen waiting for us at transfer stations around Kairos. We just happened to be in his territory."

Teknon put his hand to his forehead. The youth felt frustrated and emotionally spent. "Okay, but what about the mentors' weapons? And what kind of vitamins did you take so you could pound down that door?"

"The mentors and I invented the weapons. Each member of the team has a weapon of his own choosing and design. Arti's face band gives him the ability to immobilize individuals or groups of people. It's a morphonic ray that freezes on impact, and then acts as a tranquilizer. He has another beam that he calls his stealth ray. It reveals anything hidden by a holograph."

"And the others?" Teknon asked.

"Tor's armbands allow him to shoot a tetronic web from his hands. He can use the web either as a powerfully energized rope or as a net to catch an oncoming enemy. The beams are so strong that Tor can use them to support an entire building, if necessary.

"Epps' gloves give him the ability to make almost any human or animal docile just by touching them. A touch by Epios makes even the toughest intruder as calm as a domicat—at least for a while. And, as you know, Epps is a physician as well as an engineer. The gloves also enable him to diagnose an injury or illness just by touching the patient. After making the diagnosis, Epps can send the gloves a message to stimulate a person's immune system. In most cases, the patient is cured instantly.

"And then there's Matty. Underneath his clothes, he

wears a suit made of an interactive crystalline alloy. When Matty decides it's time, his body chemistry changes, his metabolism increases, and his molecular structure compensates to give him blinding speed. At times, he can run so fast you can't even see him. His shoes are designed to give him traction on almost any surface at any angle, and his glasses are made of a transparent metal compound. The glasses not only shield his eyes at high speeds, but the integrated sensors allow him to have 360-degree peripheral vision. He can see what's happening on every side." Kratos chuckled. "It's all stylishly coordinated, of course. You know how much Matty likes to look good."

"Of course," Teknon said, grinning. "But what about you?"

"Oh yes," Kratos replied as he put his hands behind his head, "the incident with the door. I used the Hoplon."

"How?"

"The Hoplon gives me several capabilities that are activated and controlled by the messages I send through my brain waves. When I need extra strength, I send the message, and my tissue matrix intensifies by a factor of 100. There are a few other things I can do with it. Your mentors' weapons work on the same principle of neuroresponse."

Teknon was quiet for a minute. "You created these marvels of science just for this journey, didn't you?"

"Yes," his father replied. "And now I think you should hear the rest of the story."

Teknon sat up. "You mean there's more?"

"Much more," Kratos said. "We are on a mission to retrieve something very important from my old partner, Magos. I've told you that he was evil and dangerous. But what I haven't told you is why he is what he is. It's for *that* reason that we're here."

"I'm all ears."

"Years ago, the people of Basileia abandoned the strong principles and values they once embraced. Because they had no more battles to fight after the defeat of the Daimons, they also had nothing to reinforce their need for pure living. They became complacent, and leisure became the focal point of their existence. Technology also increased at a tremendous rate. Crude entertainment and crime began to flourish.

"That's where Magos and I came in. Twenty years ago, we were the pride of the Military Technology Development Program. The high officials considered us protégés and put all of their resources at our disposal. They knew if they gave us enough freedom, we could create weaponry powerful enough to contain the growing violence that had erupted throughout Basileia.

"Magos and I developed the weapons, of course. That was our job. But we wanted to create something more, something that would contribute to the quality of life for Basileians. We hoped that by channeling some of our efforts toward this kind of project, we could use our gifts more productively. Ultimately that didn't occur."

"What happened?" asked Teknon.

"We developed a biosynthetic matrix that allowed terminally ill patients the opportunity to replace diseased organs or limbs with new ones. We could create arms, legs, and even internal organs that performed far beyond conventional physical capabilities. I was thrilled with the tests. Magos, likewise, celebrated our breakthrough. Unfortunately, he began to see another vision for our invention.

"Even though we were considered geniuses, we still struggled with the immaturity of our youth. When Magos saw the potential of biosynthetic replacement, he envisioned himself in a new hybrid body of man and machine. Magos saw the possibility of no disease or muscular deterioration. Immortality, he thought, was within his grasp. Over a period of time, without my knowledge or consent, Magos created a new body for himself. Then one very dark day, he used the master computer to interface his new hybrid body with the neurosynaptic responses of his brain. A subtle flaw in the programming caused the computer to intermix its circuitry with Magos' brain waves. The result was terrible.

"Magos became a hybrid, all right, but not as he had hoped. He was now more machine than man—a brilliant creation, but without a conscience. He acquired more data than he had ever thought possible. The more Magos knew, the more he wanted to know. He craved power, and he enjoyed devising evil strategies to get it. With his mind warped and calculating, he grew callous, and evil.

"When he came to me in his new condition, I couldn't believe what I saw. He was a foot taller than before, broad and strong. Although his face retained its former likeness, the rest of him looked like a human fortress. Cables seemed to erupt from his head, and his right eye had been replaced with an optical implant. His right ear was also missing, now replaced with a small, intricate antenna.

"Magos offered to recreate me as he had himself, but I refused. He was furious and could have killed me on the spot, but he didn't. As he left the complex, the guards tried to stop him. He used an internal force field that was now a part of his new body. The guards flew back like feathers swept in a windstorm. He never returned after that."

"How do you know he's here on Kairos?" Teknon asked.

"Over the years I've received reports from our allies about his influence on Kairos. I think he has allowed me to get those reports just so I could know where he was in case I decided to join him. You see, Teknon, Magos isn't interested in creating an army to conquer Kairos or take Basileia by force, as the Daimons once did. He knows that if he destroys the values of our society, he can rule through an underground of evil.

"Magos is behind the recent, heightened growth of sensuality and materialism on Basileia. He knows that if the people get focused on themselves and their own pleasures, they'll lose sight of what's really important—obeying Pneuma and serving others. Then the very fabric of our civilization will tear apart at the seams. He uses creations like Scandalon to tempt and seduce people.

He has established his headquarters here on Kairos, building his android army and slowly infiltrating our home planet until the day when he will dominate it completely. Where there is no character, there is no threat to Magos. He's hoped for many years that I would abandon my character and

beliefs to join him. Although he would like me to be his partner again, he loathes me as his mortal en-emy because I will
not give in. But I will not allow him either to rule or ruin
Basileia." Kratos sat up, visibly unsettled.

Teknon spoke. "If he's as brilliant and powerful as you
say, how do you hope to defeat him?"

"For the past 20 years, I've researched the teachings and
fighting strategies of the CHAMPION Warriors. My parents
began that process when I was young. Later, after Magos'
transformation, I became consumed to learn all that I could
about that forgotten league of heroes. At first, it was difficult
for me even to find anything containing the Warrior codes for
living. But I kept searching until I found what remained of
their teaching files.

"As you know, I became very successful in my work. But I
decided early in my career that my financial gains would only
serve to support my overall goals and vision. My inventions
and patents provided funds for my research and training. In
my studies, I found that the original Warriors lived by a
creed. They called it the CHAMPION Warrior Creed. The
first letters of the key words spell out the word CHAMPION
when they are combined together. It went:

> 'If I have the Courage to face my fears; Honor,
> which I show to Pneuma and my fellow man; the
> proper Attitude concerning myself and my circum-
> stances; the Mental Toughness required to make hard
> decisions; Purity of heart, mind, and body; the
> Integrity to stand for what I believe, even in the most
> difficult situations; effective Ownership of all that is
> entrusted to me; and focused Navigation in order to
> successfully chart my course in life; I will live as a
> true CHAMPION Warrior, committed to battling evil,
> and changing my world for Pneuma's glory.'

"Eventually, I learned not only how to live and think as a
CHAMPION Warrior, but I also learned how to fight like one.
When Magos and I parted ways, I took a research trip to the

Mache Region. That's where I met your mentors. The Maches were the only tribe on Basileia that continued to practice amuno, the old CHAMPION style of hand-to-hand combat. It's difficult to learn, but highly effective. During the past two decades, they have taught me all they know about amuno.

"Your mother, who shares my love for Basileia and the CHAMPION principles, has been more than patient with me during the past 20 years. My training took much time and effort, but she stood with me as my soul mate during the entire process. I could never have accomplished so much without her." Kratos' voice broke a bit. He paused to take a deep breath and continued, "I intentionally shielded you as much as possible from my quest to become a CHAMPION Warrior. Only your mother and your mentors knew of our plan. I wanted to wait until you reached the appropriate level of maturity to share it with you.

"And that, Teknon, leads me to the present day. We have a challenge far greater than anything you or I have ever faced. I brought you here because it's time I taught you how to become a CHAMPION Warrior. Basileia's future is at stake, and we, along with your mentors and a growing number of people on our home planet, are its only hope. The rigorous physical training you've undertaken is only the beginning. I will begin to teach you what I have learned, and you can join me as we face Magos."

Kratos stood up. He drew himself to his full height and spoke to his son in a solemn tone. "I ask you now, Teknon, are you with me in this?"

Teknon hesitated, then stood up to face Kratos. He clenched his jaw and responded to his father's challenge. "One hundred percent!" he exclaimed.

"It will be difficult, but the result will be worth our effort. Our mission is clear. The Logos, which is the monument to the CHAMPION Warriors and archive of all of their teachings, is in Magos' possession. He stole it years ago to remove any memory of the life once lived on Basileia. You, your mentors, and I must retrieve it. If we are successful, we can take the Logos back to its proper home. By doing this we will encourage the growing number of supporters of CHAMPION living on Basileia. A new era will begin!"

"I'm ready now," Teknon urged. "Let's go get it!"

"We've got a lot of ground to cover before then. And you have a great deal of training to do. We will rendezvous with the mentors in seven days. At that point, we will reassess our strategy and proceed. But we will face many obstacles on this mission and probably several temptations designed to interrupt our focus. Just remember, Teknon, no matter what happens, as you become a CHAMPION Warrior you will win or lose by the way you choose."

"Sounds great!" Teknon replied.

"It's not going to be easy for you, Son," Kratos cautioned. "Your belief in Pneuma is shaky at best, and you must become united with Him if you're going to become a CHAMPION. He will fill and empower you if you let Him. The challenges ahead are great and the stakes are high. I only hope you can learn quickly."

Teknon's energy surged as the impact of his dad's information sank in. This is the real thing, he thought. *An important challenge that Dad and I can face together.* Then a different thought popped into his head. He turned to Kratos. "Did you say Scandalon was Magos' *second* most dangerous android?"

Kratos nodded. "Magos has a permanent guard keeping watch over the Logos. His name is Dolios. Not only must we defeat Scandalon, we will eventually battle Dolios."

"What's Dolios like?" Teknon asked. "I mean, what makes him so dangerous?"

Kratos answered. "Magos programmed Dolios with the ability to sense and identify his opponent's greatest fears. Once identified, Dolios can take the form of that which frightens his enemy the most."

"What would that be for us?" Teknon said.

"It's individual. You may not even know what it is," Kratos warned. "Your greatest fear may be buried somewhere in your subconscious mind. But Dolios will know, and he will take advantage of your greatest fear to defeat you. That's why we must prepare mentally, emotionally, physically, and especially spiritually before we meet him. Only then can we hope for victory. Are you still with me?"

"Of course," Teknon replied. "So when does my training begin?"

"Tomorrow morning, bright and early."

"In that case," Teknon said, hoping to sound more tired than he was, "I think I'll get some sleep."

"Not quite yet, my boy," Kratos said, pulling at his son's shoulder.

Teknon winced. "The Shocktech?"

"The Shocktech," Kratos responded. "Now tell me, why in the world did you spend most of your money on something as useless as a Shocktech?"

"I felt like I needed a weapon," Teknon explained. "You and the other guys have weapons. Don't you think I need one, too?"

Kratos shook his head, then smiled slightly. "All right, let's first discuss the difference between a *need* and a *want*. Considering the arsenal that the rest of our team possesses, why do you feel that you need a Shocktech?"

"Well, I ... " Teknon hesitated.

Kratos pushed on. "And considering the fact that the Shocktech is basically an offensive weapon, not defensive, why do you want one?"

Teknon reached into his bag and pulled out the chrome weapon. "I guess I really wouldn't want to use it on someone."

"Then the Shocktech was really a *want*, wasn't it?" Kratos asked. "It looked good, felt good, and it made you feel better, right?"

Teknon nodded.

"You got caught up in the moment and purchased it impulsively."

Again Teknon agreed.

"Lesson number one in CHAMPION training: Ownership. Use your resources wisely. Try not to purchase impulsively. When you're entrusted with resources, even those you've earned yourself, learn to ask yourself, 'Do I really need this?'

You can splurge once in a while, but give yourself enough time to think about it before you make the purchase. Agreed?"

"Agreed," Teknon replied. Then he took a long glance at the Shocktech. "Y'know, now that I've had time to think about it, I can't believe I almost emptied my entire purse on it."

"When we get deep into the forest," Kratos said, "I'll show you something else you may not know about the Shocktech. But for now, let's get some sleep."

Teknon returned to his mat, and everything became quiet. Several minutes went by before Teknon finally broke the silence and asked, "By the way, how do you know so much about Shocktechs?"

"I bought one when I was about your age," his father chuckled.

"How much did you pay for it?" Teknon asked.

"Let's just say it was too much," Kratos responded.

Teknon rolled over with a smile and went to sleep.

THE SECOND LOOK

K ratos and Teknon pressed on through the dense
Forest of Perasmos surrounded by a canopy of lush
vegetation and wildlife. It rained almost constantly, and
when the rain stopped the hot air was still thick with mois-
ture. At the end of the third day, both travelers felt weary
and needed refreshment. Tired of dehydrated rations, Kratos
decided to pick edible greenery and trap small animals for
meat.

Kratos set the Hoplon on scan and took the first reading.
"Look at this, Teknon. There's a fresh, spring-fed pool about
500 meters due west. I don't know about you, but I'm feeling
about as ripe as a newborn sandsnipe." He stood up and
wiped his brow. "Why don't we set camp and take a swim
before dinner?"

Teknon put his pack down and stretched his back. "I can't
think of anything that would feel better. I'm ready for a
plunge right now. Let's get to it."

Teknon started to reach for the sleeping pads when Kratos
stopped him. "Tell you what, Son. I'll take care of setup. I've

pushed you pretty hard during the last few days, and you haven't complained once. Head over to the pool, and I'll be there directly."

"Are you sure?" Teknon's voice picked up. "I'll be glad to help."

"Go on," Kratos interrupted. "If you don't hurry, I may beat you there."

"Even Matty and his new designer threads wouldn't stand a chance," Teknon said, stretching into long strides and breaking a sweat as he hurried toward the water's edge.

He prepared for a spread-eagled dive into the inviting pool, but stopped abruptly and ducked behind some bushes. *Someone is already swimming,* he thought as he peered through the leaves. Teknon tried to focus on the stranger. Near the far edge of the pool, a young Perasmian forest dweller about Teknon's age was finishing her swim and leaving the water. As she stepped out of the pool, Teknon could see that her bathing suit didn't cover very much of her well-formed and attractive body.

At first he thought about turning away and going back to camp. But he didn't. He continued to watch the young woman as she dried off. He bent lower behind a bush, still able to keep her in sight. His heart beat faster, and his mouth dried. "She's beautiful," Teknon whispered.

Finally she disappeared into the forest on the other side of the pool. Teknon, regaining his composure, felt strange. He didn't know why he hadn't let her know he was there or why he didn't just go back and wait for his father. Shaking his head, he turned around to return to camp. He stopped short. In front of him, face-to-face, stood the Perasmian maiden. Teknon, startled and embarrassed, tried to talk. "Hello. I was just ... where did you come from? My name is Teknon."

"Hello, Teknon," the young woman said in a calm and friendly voice. "My name is Apoplanao, but my friends call me Lana."

"Hi, Lana," Teknon said, still fumbling for words but regaining a few of his wits. He looked over to the other side of the pool. "Say, how did you get from over there so ... ?" He stopped and stared at her. Her nearly naked body was still wet, and she was smiling at him. She was also standing uncomfortably close. He felt strange—uneasy and thrilled at the same time. His heart began to race, and he didn't know what to do. Should he excuse himself, or should he try to get to know her better? Something told him that he should leave, but he didn't move.

"I've just had a swim in the pool over there," she said. "It's called The Eye of Perasmos." She smiled and continued, "I just got out, but you already knew that. I saw you watching me."

Teknon blushed and tried to recover. "Well, yeah, I mean I was just coming to take a swim myself. My father and I have been walking for several days, and ... "

"Where is your father now?" Lana asked.

"He's setting up camp," Teknon responded. "He'll be here in a little while."

"Well, why don't we go back to the Eye?" she said, taking Teknon by the arm and motioning toward the spring. "I can stay a little longer."

"Well, maybe I should wait." Teknon started to pull back.

Lana gave him a gentle tug. "Your father will be here soon. Come, I'll show you where the water erupts through the sand. It's beautiful."

Teknon hesitated, then nodded. "Okay," he said, and they walked to the water.

Teknon enjoyed talking with her as they splashed in the beautiful pool. He felt like he was getting to know her very quickly; already she seemed like a friend. He couldn't believe how familiar and pleasant she was. Teknon relaxed as he swam on his back, talking about the skirmish and escape in Kopto. Suddenly he noticed that she was standing directly over him! Her face was almost touching his. He could tell that she was going to kiss him. Again, he felt like he should move, swim underwater, or do something. But he didn't. Her face was getting closer.

Suddenly a familiar voice from the other side of the pond called out, "Teknon! Here I am!" Lana pulled back, and Teknon's face submerged. He came up snorting and coughing. By the time Teknon stood up, Kratos was close at hand, but Lana was nowhere in sight.

"Dad," Teknon said, looking around. "Hey—where is she?"

"Gone," Kratos replied, eyes fixed on his son. "It looked like quite a friendly scene from where I was standing."
Kratos looked directly into his son's eyes.

Teknon was dizzy and embarrassed. "I'm not sure what happened," he explained as he pushed back his wet hair. "One minute we were laughing and waiting for you. The next ... "

"What's her name?" Kratos asked.

"Lana," Teknon said. "I guess she must live somewhere around here."

"No," Kratos said, "her name is not Lana and she's not from around here."

"What are you talking about, Dad?" Teknon blurted out.

"It was Scandalon," Kratos said. "I told you he could take any form that would cause us the greatest amount of damage. When you left camp, I noticed that there were no life forms registering on the Hoplon. But there were fibronic emissions coming from the pool. All of the creatures that Magos creates are based in a synthetic, fibronic structure. When I saw that, I knew Scandalon must be close by."

Teknon walked to the shore of the pool and sat down. His dizziness slowly turned to anger. "So that stupid android has been watching us the entire time we've been here." He hit his forehead with his hand. "How idiotic can I get?"

Kratos helped Teknon to his feet, and they walked back to camp in silence.

Later, after a leafy dinner of the local vegetation, Kratos mixed a container of nela using cool spring water he brought back from the pool. He filled two cups and sat down next to Teknon. Teknon felt the cool sides of the cup and smelled the soothing aroma of the nela.

"Scandalon dresses up pretty well, wouldn't you say?" Kratos said smiling.

"I still can't believe it," Teknon said. "I lost all control. I even forgot you were coming to join us. What was Scandalon trying to do?"

Kratos stood up, went over to Teknon's bag, and pulled out the Shocktech. "Come with me," Kratos ordered. Teknon put down his cup and followed his father to a clearing within the light containment field.

"Do you remember when I said I would show you something interesting about the Shocktech?" Kratos positioned his fingers inside the holes of the weapon.

"Yes," Teknon said. "What is it?" He watched his father aim at a large X that had been carved into a tree at the edge of the light.

"Do you think I'm a good shot?" Kratos asked, as he balanced the Shocktech with his other hand.

"You know I do," Teknon responded. "Who wouldn't? Arti says you could hit a digmite at a hundred meters." Kratos squinted, then slowly pulled the trigger. The thin beam of the Shocktech grazed a branch and traced past the tree, missing the X entirely. Teknon couldn't believe it!

"You better lay off the nela, Dad," Teknon said wryly. "How in the world could you miss a target like that?" Kratos lowered his hand and released his grip on the Shocktech.

"The Shocktech is a fine-looking piece," Kratos said, giving the weapon back to Teknon, "but it has one design flaw. It's made by Kaironians for Kaironians. Their vision base has a two-degree variance from that of Basileians. Even if I aim at the target correctly, I'll still miss it."

"But you missed it completely," Teknon said. "If the variance is just two degrees, why was your shot so bad?"

Kratos looked at Teknon. "A universal principle, Son: Error increases with distance. If I'm off, even by a fraction, at the beginning of my shot, by the time the beam reaches the target I'll miss it entirely. My aim must be completely in line with the target from the outset. It's kind of like your experience today."

Teknon closed his eyes. He knew what was coming. "Uh, oh," Teknon said.

"CHAMPION topic of the day: Purity," Kratos said.

"Dad, c'mon. Nothing happened," Teknon whined. "She skipped out when you came along. Anyway, it wasn't even a

girl." Teknon's shoulders slumped as he put his hands on his hips. "What a weird day this turned out to be."

Kratos responded, "Teknon, I realize what happened today was a frustrating and embarrassing experience for you. But if you can learn from it, you will understand where to stop the process in a similar situation. When you face another temptation like that, you'll be able to make the right choice at the right time."

"Right time?" Teknon inquired.

Kratos clarified his statement. "Let's say you're riding in a transtron racer. Your speed is factor 12. You see a cliff ahead with a drop of several thousand meters. When should you think about slowing down?"

"Well, if I know the cliff is ahead," replied Teknon, "I've got to apply thrusters immediately."

"Exactly!" Kratos exclaimed. "So when do you think you should start planning to prevent another situation like today?"

"Now, I suppose," Teknon said quietly. "I need to decide what I would do now, rather than later, in case something like that happens again." He paused. "I guess I shouldn't have taken the second look."

"Second look?" Kratos asked.

"When I saw her swimming," Teknon said, "my first thought was to come back to camp. I started to turn around, but I took a second look. I stayed after that and let my mind start wandering."

"And she almost kissed you, didn't she?" Kratos asked.

"Yeah," said Teknon. "It happened pretty fast."

"Teknon," Kratos said, "you were created with certain desires. There is nothing strange or unhealthy about wanting to kiss a woman. Physical attraction between a man and a woman is normal. But physical intimacy was created for marriage. In marriage, sex is a wonderful thing. It provides the ultimate emotional, physical, and spiritual bond between two people in this lifetime. If a couple will wait to experience sex in the correct setting of marriage, they will receive incredible benefits of trust, bonding, and sheer enjoyment. However, if sex is misused, many long-term problems can occur."

"But nothing happened," Teknon insisted.

"My point is this," continued Kratos. "Any step you take in the direction of physical intimacy, even holding hands or kissing, is the first step along a road that can only find its completion in marriage. It's like the cliff. Once you take a step closer to the edge, it's very difficult to take a step back. Remember the Shocktech? Error increases with distance. Right now you're aiming directly at the target of physical purity in your life. But if you make choices toward a physical relationship now, it will be harder and harder to stop the momentum in the future."

"So what are you saying?" asked Teknon. "Do you want me to stay away from women completely until I'm ready to get married?"

"Of course not," replied his father. "Have friends and learn to respect women correctly. But keep a tight rein on your mind, your heart, and your body. Develop the convictions to make the right decisions ahead of time." Kratos paused for a moment, then squinted his eyes and rubbed his hand across his forehead. Then he looked at his son. "Teknon, I'm going to recommend a very high standard of conduct for you to follow."

"Okay," Teknon said, a bit skeptical. "What do you have in mind?"

"According to my research," Kratos continued, "the CHAMPION Warriors made a radical commitment that they would not kiss a woman until marriage. They called it the 'Wedding Kiss.' They decided to raise their standard of purity so they could save themselves completely for their spouse. How does that strike you?"

"Wait until marriage to kiss a woman?" Teknon said, surprised. "Don't I need to go into the 'big M' with a little practice?"

"Some things you don't need to practice," Kratos said. "They just come naturally, and learning with the right person is half the fun."

"What's the other half?" Teknon asked.

"Getting better at it with the right person," Kratos said, chuckling.

"Did you and Mom wait for the Wedding Kiss?"

Kratos stopped smiling. "Unfortunately, no. Although we weren't sexually intimate, we did kiss before our wedding. I didn't even consider that waiting was an option at the time. I wasn't challenged by anyone to wait, but now I wish I had saved our first kiss for our wedding night. If I had it to do over, I would have built our dating relationship even more around deepening our friendship and less around physical attraction."

Teknon thought for several moments. "I don't know, Dad. It sounds so extreme. None of my friends are going to buy into this. How can I possibly make it that long?"

"You will receive all the divine power you need. The trick is to stay focused on the right things, set your boundaries in advance, and take precautions. Remember the Shocktech and the cliff examples. Besides, your mother and I, as well as your mentors, will encourage you every step of the way. We will also hold you accountable and remind you to keep your standard high in the area of purity."

Teknon scratched his head. "Well, maybe I need to think about this Wedding Kiss idea for a while."

"You do that," Kratos said, taking off his shirt. "Right now, I'm heading for that pool, and I'll be there before you even start thinking about how good it's going to feel."

"What's that, old man?" Teknon joked, as he threw off his shirt. "Why don't you just sit down and rest a while. I'll tell how good it felt later."

"After our swim, we'll practice some amuno," Kratos said. "I'll teach you a move we call 'the missing knee.'"

"It's got to be more effective than that Shocktech," Teknon said, turning toward the path that led to the spring.

His father, however, was already sprinting out in front.

THE COMPANY I KEEP

K ratos and Teknon paused for a moment as they looked down from the ledge. Spectacular lights caused them to blink while the thunderous fanfare of wild nightlife rose up the mountain to their ears. It had been a long week in the wilderness and there was no other city within five hours of travel. Unfortunately, Bia seemed the only alternative for a real meal and night of lodging with indoor plumbing.

"Not my choice for an evening's rest, Teknon," Kratos frowned.

"You're just hungry and tired, Dad. Two more hours on the road, and you'll be chasing spike rats again to cook for stew. I, for one, would enjoy a meal that didn't smell like the inside of my boot."

"More like the bottom of your boot," Kratos replied. "Well, a decent night's sleep and a hot bath wouldn't hurt either. But you realize, Teknon, this is Bia. We'll probably have to keep a low profile just to avoid the goings-on. There's probably not a town in the region with the reputation this place enjoys. I don't know. Maybe we should press on a bit farther."

"C'mon, Dad," Teknon pushed his father, "what's going to happen? Where's that Dolios-slayer mentality you keep telling me about?"

"This is not about courage, Son." Kratos paused and thought a moment. "So, no more spike rat stew, eh? All right, let's grab our gear and head in. I'll even spring for a keline steak dinner if you can recite the CHAMPION Warrior Creed as we walk." Teknon smiled as the two started walking toward the lights and sounds.

As they entered the small, bustling town at dusk, the smell of hot food permeated the night air. Teknon grabbed his father's arm and dragged him toward the source of the wonderful scent. The large, open door of the Revile Inn led the way to loud music and roaring laughter. Kratos pointed toward a table and motioned to the server as they sat down.

"Your specialty?" Kratos asked.

"Filet of keline, all you can eat. Two specas each."

"Sounds good," Teknon said eagerly as he sat down. "Bring it on."

The two ate ravenously, savoring every morsel. After four steak and veal plant combination platters, the long week without regular food seemed to fade into a distant memory. After dinner, the two leaned back and took a draw of their iced drink. As they relaxed, Teknon noticed a small group of young men sitting a few tables away, laughing and slapping each other on the backs. The youths were not much older than Teknon, yet they towered over him. They all wore the same sharp-looking green and dark-blue uniforms. Their handsome faces and muscular frames complemented the charismatic nature of their personalities. They each wore a beret with a red emblem in front, obviously the mark of their organization. Teknon could not keep from watching them.

"Dad, look at those guys over there." Teknon pointed.

"Hmm," Kratos responded, while placing the final fork of tiaberry pie in his mouth. He nodded in the direction of the young men. "Those guys?"

"Yeah. I don't think I've ever seen a sharper-looking group in my life. Who do you think they are? And what's with the uniforms?"

"They're Harpax," Kratos said.

Teknon swung his chair around and leaned toward his father, "Harpax? How do you know?"

Kratos sipped on his drink. "I met a few of them last year in the Mantra Quadrant. Not a very principled lot, the Harpax; they're always looking for an opportunity to cause a fight. There's a weak family structure on their planet. You often see young ones like these forming groups, trying to find a place to fit in."

"But look at them, Dad," Teknon retorted as he looked back to the Harpax table. "They look like they could take on just about anything. Nothing but ice in those veins, I'll bet. Mind if I go over and mingle with them a bit?"

Kratos peered at Teknon from the corner of his eye. "What about your sleep? We've got a long day ahead of us tomorrow."

"I won't be long. You go ahead to the room and get to bed. I'll be up soon. Okay?"

Kratos stood up slowly and stretched. "All right, Son. Remember, though, looks can be deceiving. Be careful."

"I'll be up in a few, Dad," Teknon said as his dad went up the stairs.

Teknon straightened up to his full height and walked with his most confident stride to the Harpax table. "Hi, guys," he said, "what's goin' on?"

The Harpax nearest to Teknon stood up and looked down at him. "And who might you be, little one?"

"Teknon, son of Kratos, from the planet Basileia."

"What are you doing here?" asked the Harpax.

"Just trying to fill a couple of empty stomachs," Teknon replied. "Mind if I join in the conversation?"

The huge Harpax thought for a moment, then, with toothy grin, barked at his cohorts. "Seems we have a new companion, my friends. Welcome to our table, Teknon, son of Kratos." He slapped Teknon on the back, almost knocking the wind out of him, and thrust a chair under his legs. As Teknon sat, he noticed the apparent leader of the group leaning over the table. He spoke directly to Teknon.

"My name is Rhegma and I am commander of this Harpax clan. In short, our driving purpose is to protect the town of Bia from those undesirable characters who would seek to cause chaos and disruption in our fair city. We are the guardians of the law, so to speak."

Teknon, interested by Rhegma's statement, asked him, "So you've organized a protection squad for the good of the people. Is that it?"

"Precisely. You see, Teknon, we fight for what is right. No one stands in our way, no one tells us what to do, because we stand together." Rhegma leaned back in his chair and smiled at the enthralled youth. "So, interested in joining us tonight?"

Teknon, caught off guard by the offer, responded. "What? Join you? Tonight? What do you mean, like go out and patrol the area or something?"

"Sure," Rhegma said.

"Well, I don't know," said Teknon. "I've really got to get some sleep for tomorrow's journey. I probably shouldn't stay out that late."

"Nonsense!" growled another Harpax. "What we do won't take long. Don't worry, you'll get your rest, son of Kratos," he said winking at another Harpax.

Teknon sensed that strange feeling again. His hands tingled, and his stomach turned a little. Still, he did not want to appear timid in front of this impressive group. "Okay," Teknon said, "I'll join you for a little while."

"Splendid! Gentlemen," Rhegma said, motioning to his companions, "our public awaits."

Another Harpax slapped Teknon on the back again and firmly pushed him toward the door with the rest of the group.

Outside, Teknon walked with the Harpax as they strode down the street. Shoulder to shoulder they walked, a distinctive smirk on their faces and an arrogance in their talk. Teknon was surprised to hear the foul stories his new companions so easily threw around. The Harpax cursed and laughed as they told degrading jokes about the women of Bia. Teknon felt more uncomfortable by the moment. They looked down every alley as they passed by, but Teknon did not know what they were looking for.

Suddenly, Rhegma stopped and pointed to two individuals over by a door in an alley. The leader gave a hand signal to the other Harpax as he began walking toward the people. Teknon and the other Harpax followed, staying in the shadows to prevent detection. Rhegma grabbed the first person's collar, then struck him on the neck with a well-defined blow. The victim dropped to the ground immediately. Teknon's jaw dropped when he saw that it was a boy only about 15 years old. He was shocked. The youth was hurt and unconscious.

Rhegma grinned and pointed to the other boy who was about the same age. "Caught you, didn't we?" Rhegma growled. "Thought you could get away with the store's earnings for the night." Both boys, obviously filled with terror, stepped back.

"No, no," one replied. "We work here and were just closing up. Look, here is our work card." The boy feverishly reached to his pocket to reveal his identification.

"Liar," another Harpax yelled, as he snatched the card out of the hand of the frightened youth. Then the Harpax swung a hard backhand against his face, drawing blood and knocking him down. "Where are the earnings?" the Harpax yelled.

"They're inside," said the boy, holding his nose with both hands and grimacing. "We lock them in the container field every night."

"And you have the combination, I suppose?" Rhegma said slowly, pulling his gloves on tightly.

"Yes, I do," said the youth, trembling.

"Well then," replied Rhegma, "why don't we take a trip into your store and see just how well you know that locking sequence."

Teknon got the picture all too clearly, but also all too late. "Wait a minute, Rhegma, what are you doing?" he said. "I thought you were here to protect the public, not vandalize it. Let these guys go. Why don't you get out of here before the real authorities arrive and cart you away?!" Teknon just wanted to get the Harpax away from the youths so that he could help them. Suddenly a large Harpax grabbed Teknon by the collar and raised his massive fist in the air.

"Looks like our new member is bailing out, Rhegma. How 'bout a little parting gift for this house pet?"

"Fine," Rhegma said without expression or emotion. "Do it, and let's get inside." The Harpax holding Teknon grinned as he raised his fist higher.

The movement of a figure from the shadows was so fast that no one knew he was there until they heard the sound of metal connecting with the back of a Harpax head. The Harpax holding Teknon immediately shrieked in pain and released his grip.

In a split second, the group heard another sound—the thump of the shield returning to Kratos' hand. Teknon saw the clear outline of his father's silhouette in the light of an alley lamp, shield in hand and ready for battle. Another Harpax lunged at him, but Kratos gracefully stepped aside, placing a well-focused kick on the knee of the huge youth. The Harpax dropped to the ground, gripping his leg and groaning.

"Any others?" Kratos chided. "How about you, Rhegma?"

Rhegma, regaining his composure, offered an evil grin. He turned toward Teknon and said, "Another day, small one." Then Rhegma looked back at Kratos. "Another day." With that, Rhegma instructed his followers to assist their wounded accomplices, and they vanished quickly into the darkness.

Kratos placed the shield back onto its harness, and kneeled down to help the injured young man, now conscious. As his father helped the youth to his feet, Teknon spoke. "How did you know? Why did you let me go with them?"

After Kratos made sure the young man was able to walk home with his friends, one of the boys turned and shook his hand warmly. Then both boys ran down the alley, anxious to get home as fast as possible.

"Teknon, I told you my hesitation about coming to Bia was not about courage, remember?" Kratos replied.

"Yes," said Teknon. "What of it?"

"I knew if we came into town, you would probably meet up with one of the Harpax groups. Knowing your tendency to be impressed by outward appearance, I wanted you to see just how deceiving looks can be. Discernment is critical, Teknon. You must learn to use discernment if you are to help me defeat Magos when we meet him. If you had been using discernment, thinking wisely through your options, you would not only have avoided the Harpax but also the city of Bia. Observe all of the characteristics of a person. Don't just look at the surface. You must learn to think clearly and make wise decisions."

Teknon looked at the ground for a moment, then back at Kratos. "I blew it, didn't I? I started sensing the whole thing was a mistake, but I didn't want them to think I wasn't tough. I wanted them to like me."

"My friends are those who bring out the best in me, Teknon," Kratos said. "The Harpax always bring out the worst. Did they start using vulgar language and telling raunchy stories?"

"Yep," Teknon said, shaking his head.

"They're known for that. Remember, bad humor is a sign of bad morals."

"By the way, how did you get so close without us noticing?" Teknon asked. "It was like you just appeared from nowhere."

"I used the Hoplon," Kratos replied.

"The shield again? What did it do, make you invisible?"

"I sent it a message through my thoughts to create a holographic image that matched the background of the alley. You couldn't see me, but I was there."

"That thing is incredible. I wish I had one. Anyone ever tell you that you're a genius?"

"Not today," Kratos said, smiling. "The Hoplon is only a tool, Teknon, but a tool that requires great responsibility from its owner to use it correctly. Can you imagine the Hoplon in the wrong hands?"

"You mean Magos?" Teknon asked.

"Well, certainly Magos. But Magos has his own tools that

he uses for destruction. I'm talking about someone else who could begin with the right motives, but lose his way to evil because of the temptation of power. Few people can handle power without misusing it."

"You know, Dad, life is tough. But when you're stupid, like I was tonight, it's a lot tougher. I should have listened to your advice."

Kratos smiled and put his arm around his son's shoulder. "We're going to meet a lot of interesting people during this journey. But don't get impressed so easily; appearances can be deceiving. Trying to be liked by the wrong people will drag you down. I've found over the years that it's better to be trusted and respected than it is to be liked. Now, learn from this mistake and let's move on."

Teknon lifted his head and nodded. He felt weary and was ready to end the day. He walked and talked with his father on the way back to the lodge. As they entered their rented room, Teknon could barely keep his eyes open. He stumbled to his bed and began removing his shoes.

"Let's get to sleep," Kratos advised, "then it's back on the road tomorrow."

Teknon sighed in agreement, then said, "Just one more thing, Dad."

"Yes?" Kratos responded, lying down on his comfortable bed.

"Could we have one final meal in the morning before we get back to a regular diet of spike rat stew?"

ERGO·NIAN PRIDE

After leaving Bia, Kratos and Teknon hiked into the Plutos Region. They hoped to reach the Hudor Sea at midweek by spending long hours on foot, pushing forward with little rest. The going would have been rougher if the two were still in the hot and humid Forest of Perasmos. But the climate in this territory, with its open fields of high grass filled with exotic plant life, was far more appealing. Fruit was plentiful, and they found little need to use up their rations.

At dusk on the third day, they came to a valley that stretched toward a large body of water in the distance. The terrain was beautiful and the weather constantly pleasant. This was the "low country," as the locals called it. Snowcapped mountains towered to the east, and the shoreline of Hudor Sea lay at their southern base. Teknon smiled at his father in silent satisfaction as they reached their destination on schedule. They walked briskly down the hillside to the town of Ergo.

Thousands of Kaironians visited Ergo every year due to its appeal as a lush vacation resort. Years earlier, the residents abandoned their calm existence as farmers of the most fertile soil on Kairos. They chose instead to capitalize on the valley's perfect climate and beautiful coastline by building an incredible "holiday haven." An expensive entry pass purchased at the gate of the city provided all of the food, activities, and entertainment that anyone could ask for. The Ergonians, although pleasant and accommodating, had developed an arrogant attitude of self-sufficiency. They were a wealthy people, resistant to outsiders who wanted to offer anything except an admission price to enter their refuge.

Since their stay in Bia, Teknon and Kratos spent much of their travel time discussing the methods of amuno, the fighting style of the CHAMPION Warriors. As they walked, Kratos would describe a technique and then stop to show Teknon how it worked. Teknon also listened to his father emphasize that amuno should only be used in self-defense. In fact, Kratos explained often that amuno worked best when an opponent made the first move of aggression. Teknon learned slowly, but he remained intent on becoming adept at this new and exciting skill. The father and son also kept an eye out for the mentors. Plan C-3, which Kratos had yelled to his team in Kopto, meant that all members would rendezvous in Ergo to catch a ship across the Hudor Sea.

As Kratos and Teknon approached the gate of Ergo, the Kaironian sun was setting and the twin moons had begun their climb into the evening sky. Teknon stopped to look at the lavish entry to the city and marveled as he scanned the wall of grimstone—10 meters high and three meters thick—that surrounded Ergo. He also noticed that the wall was constructed in the shape of a U so that the ends could extend almost 200 meters into the sea.

"This place is unbelievable," Teknon marveled. "Look at that wall. Ergo isn't a resort—it's a fortress."

"At least it looks that way," Kratos replied as he reached for the money compartment of his uniform.

"What do you mean?" Teknon asked. "How much more protection from the nonpaying public can you get?"

"Every stronghold has its weakness," Kratos responded as the gate attendant began to question him.

"Which length of passport to ecstasy would you prefer, my friend?" the well-dressed Ergonian asked. "We offer a one-day, two-day, three-day, or our deluxe week-long passport."

"Two days will be plenty," Kratos said, putting the currency into the attendant's hand. "By the way, can you tell me where I can purchase passes for a ship to the other coast?"

"Why, certainly," the attendant said. "You can get them right here. Will that be first class or standard fair?"

"Standard. When does the ship leave?"

"The *Ergonaut* departs every afternoon at sundown at the pier. But don't be late."

Kratos nodded, received his change, and motioned to Teknon. "Why don't we go inside and see what 'Ergomania' is all about." The two entered through the huge armored gate and into the land of fantasy.

The village of Ergo was beautiful. Even the sidewalks looked as if they were lined with precious stones. People moved from place to place using transportation platforms that responded to verbal commands and took them to various restaurants, spas, and nightspots. Tropical music played throughout the community producing the atmosphere of a calm, secure paradise.

Teknon and Kratos rented a room at the hotel and went downstairs to the poolside restaurant to relax. Teknon noticed that many people were drinking a substance called gleukos, a sweet-tasting, aromatic potion that numbed the senses and caused the drinker to temporarily lose touch with reality.

"Why do they drink that stuff?" Teknon asked as he munched on snacks.

"This is a place to escape," Kratos said, taking a bite of a sandwich. "For a few days, all these people want to do is to forget about their lives at home. Sun, fun, eating, and drinking gleukos is what this place is all about."

"Who needs it? If I stayed here, I'd rather keep a clear head and go hoversailing," Teknon said. Suddenly a frantic Ergonian darted past their table and into the lobby of the hotel. A loud discussion occurred at the hotel desk, and the frantic man began yelling.

"Listen to that!" Teknon said, leaning forward to get a better look. "Why don't we go see what the fuss is about?"

"All right," Kratos said, "let's have a look. But we also need to start looking for the mentors. Ergo isn't that big of a place. We should be able to find them if they're here."

Kratos and Teknon went inside and listened to the loud conversation. The skittish Ergonian was trying to describe that a pack of amachos had been spotted outside of the city. They were wreaking havoc throughout the valley, killing livestock and raiding homes for food.

Amachos were dangerous creatures. Approximately three meters high, these two-legged beasts were covered with thick, matted fur. Although the amachos walked upright like humans, their destructive and savage behavior revealed a more bestial existence. They used long fangs to rip through the hide of any domestic animal, yet they had adequate intelligence to cause aggravation and harm to people. Their most menacing feature was a barbed tail that they used to snap like a whip at their prey. The barb delivered a neurotoxin that caused high fever and progressive paralysis over the course of several days until, finally, the victim could no longer move his body from the neck down. When traveling in a pack, usually 15 or more, the amachos caused great damage and injury to any community that came into their path.

"What are we going to do?!" said the Ergonian, excitedly. "We have no defenses around here. The last time we were threatened—."

Another Ergonian entered the room from a large office stationed by the hotel desk. He was tall, tan, and dressed better than the other employees. With an air of authority, he calmly interrupted the conversation. "Threatened, Mr. Strene?" he asked with a poised but angry tone of voice. He walked over to the agitated individual, who now looked frightened.

"Mr. Poroo," Strene said, hesitating, "amachos can be dangerous. Shouldn't we alert the people that ... "

"Have you lost your mind?" Mr. Poroo hissed, grabbing his anxious employee firmly by the arm. "Do you know how fast this place will empty if we tell them there's a pack of amachos nearby?" He threw Strene's arm aside in disgust. "Besides, what harm can a few oversized fur mongrels do to us inside the wall? What are they going to do, crawl over? We have the entire exterior charged with static energy when the sun goes down. And they won't try to go around the wall because they hate water. Now, stop this ridiculous cackling or I'll throw you outside the wall myself." As Poroo straightened his well-pressed jacket and turned back toward his office, he heard a voice behind him.

"He's right, you know," Kratos said, arms crossed and leaning against the front desk. "You can't underestimate the amachos. If you've got a pack swarming around the valley, you should take precautions."

Poroo slowly turned around and forced a polite smile as he responded to Kratos. "Sir, I understand your concern, especially when someone like Mr. Strene reacts so emotionally in front of our visitors." Poroo looked angrily at the cowering Strene. "But let me assure you, our guests have no need to fear any outside threat. This resort community provides not only the finest in entertainment, but also the ultimate in protection. No one and no thing can enter this resort unless I say it can."

"Amachos are powerful, resourceful creatures, Mr. Poroo. Why don't you let my son and I gather a few of your employees and guard the perimeter of the wall, at least for tonight? That will give everyone peace of mind."

Redness rise from the base of Poroo's neck and his brow furled. "Mr ... ?"

"Kratos," Kratos said calmly.

"Mr. Kratos, just because you've paid to enter our facility does not give you the right to question our ability to take care of our guests. I'll thank you to stay out of our business of running this resort and go back to your business of having a good time." Poroo turned around with a jerk. "Good night!" With that, Poroo went into his office and slammed the door.

Teknon chuckled as the disgruntled Ergonian walked away. "Well, you can't say you didn't try. Conceited fellow, isn't he?"

Kratos frowned slightly and turned to walk away. "He thought I was threatening his authority. He let his pride get bruised. That attitude might be his undoing." Kratos put his hand on his son's shoulder. "Why don't we get some dinner and head up to bed."

"I'm right behind you," said Teknon. "By the way, do you think I might try a sip of that gleukos, just to see what it's like?" Kratos turned his head and raised one eyebrow.

"Didn't think so," Teknon said.

*   *   *

Later that evening, a young couple walked hand-in-hand along a secluded path beside the wall of Ergo. As they paused to sit on a cushioned bench, they heard a strange scratching sound near the wall. At first they took no notice, but soon the noise grew stronger. In a few moments, the couple heard low, throaty growls—animal-like yet almost sounding like two people talking. The two got up and walked closer to the wall. Suddenly the earth broke open. Several hairy hands with long, sharp claws viciously tore their way through the holes.

The couple stumbled back in fear, facing several towering creatures standing upright. Their sharp teeth and glaring yellow eyes gleamed in the moonlight. Before the couple could scream, two long whip-like tails quickly snap-ped around and stung them on the neck. They crumpled instantly.

The amachos darted silently through the streets until they reached the hotel. Bursting inside, the pack leader let out a howling screech, igniting the rest of the beasts in a flurry of violence and mayhem. Hotel residents, previously enjoying a late dinner in the restaurant, screamed as amachos turned over tables and chairs. They grabbed food and began shoving it into their mouths, while at the same time snapping their tails and stinging many of the helpless resort guests.

One Ergo employee had the presence of mind to push a button behind the front desk, triggering a seldom-used alarm.

Seconds later, Poroo ran into the large room, dressed in shorts and a robe. "What's going on here?!" he yelled as he watched an amacho swilling and spilling a bottle of gleukos while stinging a fleeing guest. Poroo covered his face in terror as he saw another creature leap toward him, fangs bared.

Suddenly the amacho dropped to the ground at Poroo's feet, knocked unconscious by a round object that sliced through the air.

As soon as the Hoplon returned to Kratos, he immediately threw it again. This time it bounced off the heads of two other amachos before it returned. Another of the beasts charged Kratos. His medallion blazing, Kratos gracefully stepped aside, grabbed the creature's shoulder, pulled down, and placed a knee swiftly into its furry nose. The creature howled in pain as it grabbed its face and dropped to the floor.

When the pack leader saw Kratos, its yellow eyes narrowed and lips dripped gleukos and saliva as it prepared to pounce on the brave stranger. At that moment the amacho felt a rush of wind blow into its face, as if something had just passed by. Immediately the pack leader felt a smash to his jagged-toothed jaw, throwing the beast backward. Another blow came, this time to the stomach, but the creature still couldn't see who or what had delivered the blow. One more crash to the chin, and the leader fell limp to the ground. A figure blurred in front of the beast, then halted. Kratos saw who it was and immediately responded.

"Matty!" Kratos yelled across the room.

"At your service, Captain," Matty replied with a cocky salute. "Excuse me while I round up a few more of these oversized spike rats." Matty grabbed a heavy chain that sectioned off one of the rooms in the restaurant. In a split second, he surrounded two more amachos, bound their arms and legs, and left them in the middle of the lobby.

A hideous roar erupted outside the hotel. The remaining amachos heard the noise and froze in panic. A two-headed reptile nearly seven meters tall exploded through the lobby toward the amachos. The towering monster's eyes blazed red as it lumbered toward its prey. The amachos, tired of battling Kratos and Matty, picked up their wounded and ran at the sight of this new opponent. They scurried back through the hole under the wall until the last one was gone.

Matty stopped by Kratos' side. The two grabbed each other by the shoulders with a warm greeting.

"You sure do conjure up a mean holographic image with that shield of yours, Kratos," Matty said, laughing. "What made you decide on a phago?"

"Phagos are a natural enemy of the amachos," Kratos replied. He put the Hoplon back into the harness. "I think the amachos decided they would rather get their meal somewhere else than become a meal themselves."

Teknon stumbled down the stairs. "What's going on here?" He looked over and saw his mentor. "Hey, Matty, great to see you. How are ya?"

"Streakin', Tek. Just thought I'd zip in for a little fun with your dad." Matty walked over and slapped Teknon on the back.

"Where are the other guys?" Kratos asked.

"Haven't seen them yet," Matty replied. "I thought you all would be here by now."

Medical personnel from the resort were already helping the injured guests by injecting them with antitoxin to counteract the amacho stings. Poroo stumbled over to his two new heroes, one hand on his head. He was shaken and a bit more humble than before. "I see you were right, Mr. Kratos. I suppose I owe you an apology."

"You may owe me an apology, Mr. Poroo, but you owe your visitors a lot more. This attack could have been much worse," Kratos said.

"I'm thinking Kratos probably saved the rest of your tourist season," Matty said, walking behind Poroo and getting a dessert from the half-destroyed buffet.

"I realize that," Poroo said. "How can I repay you, Mr. Kratos? And your swift friend too, of course."

"Mr. Poroo, a wise man once said, 'A good scare is sometimes worth more than good advice,'" Kratos answered. "If you will change your attitude and fortify this place, we'll be just fine. Start taking a little advice now and then. Remember, though, the amachos aren't smart enough to know when to quit. If I were you, I'd start remodeling this place—especially the perimeter wall—as soon as possible."

"Right away," Poroo said meekly. "And thank you again." As he walked toward the front desk, he helped his visitors to their feet and began to make more apologies.

"Think he learned his lesson, Dad?" Teknon asked.

"I'm not sure. It's not easy becoming teachable when you're not used to it. It just goes to show that pride will eventually cause a person's downfall."

"By the way," Teknon said, frustrated, "I think I lost my Shocktech. When I heard the noise and saw that you were gone, I tried to find it. I must have lost it between here and Bia. Oh well, no big loss."

"Who knows," Matty chimed in, "you might have had the chance to tickle one of those hairy hodgebeasts with that cap gun."

"Well, enough excitement for one night," Kratos said. "Let's get some sleep and look for the other mentors tomorrow. We've all got a boat to catch."

"Aye, aye, Captain," Matty said.

A Storm of Dishonor

K ratos, Teknon, and Matty stood up after finishing an early dinner in the hotel restaurant. Time was running short, and they wanted to get to the dock in time for the launch. An automated voice announced over the sound system, "The *Ergonaut* will be leaving port shortly."

They picked up their packs by the table and waved goodbye to Mr. Poroo, who was still working out the details of cleanup from the night before. Poroo waved back warmly. Earlier in the day, Kratos and Matty both received a refund for their stay in Ergos, compliments of their new admirer.

As the three walked down to the dock, they noticed a large, familiar figure in the distance leaning against a post and looking somewhat impatient. The sight of his hairless head and abnormally broad shoulders caused Matty to smile widely. He zipped ahead and greeted his friend with repetitive slaps on the back.

"All right, all right, good to see you too, Mat," Tor said in his traditional, brusque tone. He stood straight and crossed his arms. "Where have you guys been? You don't seem to be in a hurry to get off this fat farm. I've been waiting here all morning." Matty, accustomed to his big companion's demeanor, continued to smile. Kratos and Teknon were not far behind.

"Tor!" Kratos exclaimed. "Glad you made it."

Tor's face lightened as he grabbed Teknon with one of his huge hands, effortlessly lifting him into the air. After a few seconds he put the boy down and affectionately pushed him away. "I arrived at the gate this afternoon. I looked at the passenger list for today's cruise. Any sign of Arti and Epps?"

"None," said Teknon, regaining his balance. "We hoped to see them by now. I'm glad, at least, that you showed up."

"Well," said Tor, "they'll catch up soon." He reached for his pack and threw it over his shoulder. "I would have been here sooner myself, but I got jumped by a couple of scratch-backs yesterday afternoon. They attempted to relieve me of my pack and sell me to the local slave merchant for labor."

"How many is a few?" Matty asked, chuckling.

"Oh," Tor said, looking ahead, "let's just say I took the opportunity to practice some new moves I've been working on. I didn't try to hurry."

"So the countryside is safe once again," Matty said. "Tor, the people of Ergo thank you."

Tor motioned to the ship. "Well, are we going to board the "Buffet Barge" or aren't we?"

"All aboard, gentlemen," Kratos said as the four stepped onto the transport platform and rose to the upper deck of the *Ergonaut*.

*   *   *

In a distant, secluded place, computer equipment lined the perimeter of a cavernous room. Powerful-looking beings resembling soldiers roamed the floor, while they silently programmed the machines and monitored data. The walls around the room shimmered as if they were made of crystal. Large video monitors hung from the ceiling on either side of the chamber. At the rear, a giant screen covered the wall from floor to ceiling. The large screen and monitors relayed images of various locations and people from around planet Kairos. The scenes changed every few seconds.

Finally, one image remained on the large screen in the back of the room. Soon, the two monitors on either side of the room displayed the same scene. The soldiers stopped their activity immediately, and everyone focused on the image. A computer-generated voice thundered from the large speakers, "Target, identified. I repeat, target identified."

On the upper balcony, two tall, metallic doors opened slowly on the back wall. A large, elaborate throne floated into the room on a cushion of air, one meter from the ground. A half human, half android cyborg sat on the throne, his long, mechanical hands curled over the throne's arm. A complex antenna was attached to his head. His face displayed a depraved smile, the foul expression of a bionic mind filled with the darkness of calculated evil.

"Master Magos," one of the soldiers said, looking up at the figure in the chair and pointing toward the screen, "your servant Scandalon has found them." Magos rose slowly from his perch and glared at the four individuals on the screen. Scandalon, appearing as a waiter on the *Ergonaut*, projected the precise image his master wanted to see.

*   *   *

Teknon had never sailed on a multi-level hydrovessel before. He walked on the upper deck with his father and companions, looking at the available forms of luxury entertainment. He gazed in wonder at the many foods and activities awaiting passengers during their two-day voyage to the region of Tarasso. The *Ergonaut* was designed specifically for leisure, with its large, open decks on five levels. Hydroaquatic engines, two meters below the surface of the water, provided propulsion for the huge vessel. The winds on the Hudor Sea were always light and the temperature remained constant, so no concessions were made for foul weather during the *Ergonaut*'s construction.

Each team member found his room, deposited his gear, and walked back to the upper deck for a cup of nela and some strategizing. As they sat at a table overlooking the clear, calm water, Tor began the conversation. "Things will start to heat up once we get to Tarasso. If Magos is following our position, he knows that we are getting closer to his command center. We need to be ready to respond quickly to whatever he throws at us."

"Agreed," Kratos said. "I'm sure we'll see more of the same from Scandalon and those like him. But it wouldn't surprise me if Magos becomes more obvious with his attacks. As you say, Tor, the closer we get to the target, the more we'll get hit."

Matty chimed in as he waved for more service at their table, "And when that time comes, gentlemen, we shall rise to the occasion. Until then, why don't we enjoy the humble surroundings that have been thrust upon us?"

*　　*　　*

Magos paced slowly as he watched the images Scandalon transmitted while serving Kratos. He stopped, crossed his arms, and scowled as he processed his options. His soldiers did not dare to approach him when he looked like this. The attachment on Magos' head began to glow with increasing intensity. Computers reacted, and lights flashed around the room. The robotic troops also responded, many changing their positions to different machines.

Magos' eyes lifted and his scowl slid into a sly grin. "I believe it's time for a slight deviation in the weather," he said.

*　　*　　*

Back on the *Ergonaut*, the team continued their strategic discussion. Teknon, leaning back in his chair, detached himself momentarily from the dialogue in order to enjoy the surrounding scenery. As he looked around, he noticed an adult speaking vigorously to two teens at a nearby table. One youth was approximately Teknon's age; the other was slightly younger. The man seemed frustrated.

The boys, however, were distant and indifferent, looking around and making no eye contact with the adult. Teknon watched with interest as both of them stood up, without regard for the man who was still talking, and walked to the pool without expression or emotion. The man, obviously disgusted, sat back in his chair.

"I have a confederate who will meet us in Tarasso," Kratos said in low tone. "We will need updated information as to the status of Magos' defensive capabilities. It will take us several days on foot just to get to his headquarters."

"Not for me," Matty said with a smile, as he put his hands behind his head and leaned back.

"You and that fancy suit," Tor said. "Well, I'll tell you one thing, it'll come in handy when we need to get logistical and tactical information quickly."

Teknon, one ear to the conversation at the table, was still watching the youths by the pool. They didn't seem to be getting along with their dad or each other.

"Dad, would you mind if I walked around?" Teknon asked. "I see a couple of Basileians about my age over by the pool." Kratos looked over to see the boys arguing.

"Looks like they could use a third party to mediate the conversation," Kratos responded. "Sure, go ahead. I'll catch up with you later."

Teknon walked over to the pool, where the two youths were almost at blows. When they saw Teknon, they stopped talking.

"Hi, fellas," Teknon said in a friendly voice. He stuck out his hand to the older of the two. "My name's Teknon." The youth looked at Teknon's hand suspiciously, then returned the gesture to shake. Teknon could see his acquaintance was not accustomed to shaking hands.

"I'm Pikros," the older youth responded.

"I'm Parakoe," the younger added. Neither returned a smile. Pikros looked Teknon over from head to foot. His eyes narrowed in a look of disdain. "Where did you get that outfit?" he asked. "What are you, some sort of soldier wanna-be?" He walked around Teknon and continued to scoff.

"No, stupid," Parakoe chimed in, "he's probably part of some sort of paramilitary club. Ain't that right, Dacron?"

Teknon chuckled to himself. "It's Teknon," he said. No,

actually I'm here with my dad and my mentors." Teknon motioned to the table.

"Wow," said Parakoe, eyes widening. "That's a tough-looking group." He pointed at Tor. "Look at that big guy."

"So, what are you guys doing here?" Teknon pointed to the table. "Who's that guy over there? Is that your dad?"

"Yeah, that's our old man," Parakoe responded indifferently.

"Seems like things were getting a bit testy over there," Teknon said, sitting down by the pool.

"Aw, forget about him," Pikros said, hands on his hips, looking back at his father. "He brought us on this trip because he feels guilty, that's all. He just wants to try to make up for not being around at home. He's always working." Pikros turned around and sat down with Teknon by the pool. Parakoe, in his swimsuit, decided to jump into the pool. "Now we're out here on this tub, and all he wants to do is give us orders. The jerk!"

Teknon, repelled by the youths' attitudes toward their father, listened during the next 15 minutes as the angry brothers described how much they hated being on the boat and how they weren't going to let their father think that they were enjoying any part of this trip. Pikros was mad because his dad had promised him a transtron racer for his birthday, but instead brought him on this stupid trip. He told Teknon that his mom and dad thought their kids should attend a military academy for boys. As Teknon listened, he couldn't help noticing that the sky was beginning to darken.

"I'm sick of it," Pikros said. At that moment, his brother splashed him playfully from the pool. Pikros erupted. "Hey, you nit winding loonhead! Do that again, and I'll come in there and smash that pug nose of yours."

Suddenly, thunder clapped loudly and lightening struck near the boat. The sky became almost pitch dark, and waves began to increase in size. The wind, almost nonexistent a few moments before, blew Pikros into the pool. All three youths, startled by the thunder, looked in disbelief at the sky.

"Whoa, when did that happen?" Teknon yelled over the wind.

Within seconds, the *Ergonaut* was tossed by powerful winds and battered by walls of water more than 15 meters high. Passengers scrambled to get below, but many lost their grip and fell. They slid across the deck as the ship rolled violently back and forth. Several screamed as they fell overboard and disappeared into the churning sea. Alarms sounded through the *Ergonaut*'s speakers, but few could hear them over the howling wind. Teknon fought to get back to his companions. As he reached them, he heard Kratos barking commands to Matty and Tor.

"Tor, use your braces to protect the lower decks!" Tor nodded and started battling his way to the side of the ship. Kratos pulled a small, cylindrical object from his pack and gave it to Matty.

"Mat!" Kratos called out at the top of his lungs, "help as many people to get below as you can, then take this locator beacon to the top of the ship in case we start sinking!" The beacon was designed to send a homing signal back to Kratos' house on Basileia. It would relay coordinates to Paideia so that she could send another team to rescue them if necessary. Matty's eyewear slid into place as he swiped the beacon from Kratos' hand.

"Already there, Captain!" Matty yelled as he flashed to the other side of the deck.

Kratos grabbed Teknon's arm and told him to stay close. Teknon followed his father as the two struggled toward the front of the ship. The *Ergonaut* continued to raise her nose high into the air with each wave, then crash down hard into the trough of the next wall of water. Oncoming waves continued to increase in size. Once they reached the bow, Kratos pointed Teknon to a large pole and yelled for him to hang on.

A hairline crack ran through the deck on the third level, resulting from the continual pounding of the waves. Teknon hung tightly to the pole as he watched his father turn and face the wind, the Hoplon fixed firmly on his back. Kratos braced himself against the storm as the emblem on his chest glowed. Teknon knew that an invisible force field was covering the front of the ship. He could see his father straining,

compelling the force field to increase in size and intensity. Soon waves began to explode against the invisible field 50 meters off the bow. Although the ship continued to rise and fall, the hull remained intact.

Meanwhile, Tor had his hands full keeping water from pouring into the open sides of the ship. He raised his arms, clenched his powerful fists, and began to shoot a wide beam of energy toward the lower decks. Immediately a bright wall formed around each level, creating a barrier to prevent water from coming aboard. First one, then another, and finally all the decks were surrounded. Tor gritted his teeth and held the energy matrix together with all his might.

Matty, meanwhile, had already helped more than 30 people to get below the top deck. Some of them didn't know how they got below. One minute they were hanging on for dear life, the next moment they were safe. Although confused, they were content to be out of the storm. Back and forth Matty streaked, until he had retrieved all of the remaining passengers on the upper deck.

When Matty determined that the passengers were safe, he focused on his next assignment. His technically advanced shoes allowed him to gain traction on almost any surface. Combined with speed, Matty's footwear enabled him to scale walls. He looked up to the highest point on the *Ergonaut*, right above the bridge. Without hesitation, he ran up the side of the ship, looking like a new streak of paint until he reached the top. He planted the beacon in a safe position, then zipped back down to join the others.

As Kratos, Tor, and Matty worked hard to keep the ship afloat, Teknon noticed that one passenger remained on deck, slumped and unconscious behind a chair. Matty hadn't noticed him in the confusion.

At that moment, an enormous wave smashed into the side of the ship. Teknon, gasping for air after the wave passed, tightened his grip on the pole. Kratos, temporarily stunned, regained his position and kept the force field intact. Tor emerged from the water, lasers blazing. Matty had gone below to help injured passengers. As Teknon's eyes refocused, he

"Where's Teknon?" Kratos said abruptly, as he looked toward the pole where his son was supposed to be. The mentors looked around anxiously.

"Here I am, Dad!" Teknon yelled, emerging from the laundry room. The injured man, his wound bandaged, leaned on Teknon's shoulder. Kratos and the mentors rushed to the man's side and helped him to a chair. The man looked up at Teknon and squeezed his arm with gratitude.

"My name is Ameleo," the man said to Kratos. "You must be this young man's father." Kratos nodded and looked at Teknon.

"I'm Kratos. This is Tor and Matty. What happened, Mr. Ameleo?"

"I slipped and hit my head when one of the first waves hit. The next thing I knew your son was bandaging my wound and watching out for me through the storm. I probably would have dropped overboard and drowned if not for your son's heroic efforts." Once again Ameleo looked at Teknon, then back toward Kratos. "You've got quite a boy, Mr. Kratos."

Kratos smiled with affirmation at his son while Tor raised Teknon over his head. "I guess we'll keep this kid a while longer," Tor said with a laugh. When Teknon returned to the ground, Kratos put his arm around his shoulder.

"Has anyone seen my boys?" Ameleo asked. "I don't remember them getting to safety." Just then, two familiar heads appeared from the lower deck, squinting as the sun hit their eyes.

"Pikros! Parakoe!" yelled Ameleo. "Here I am. Come over here!" The boys strolled toward their father.

"Dad," Parakoe said, "where did you go? Pikros has been hitting me for talking too much. He's been acting like a jerk."

"You spike rat!" Pikros retaliated. "When the waves came, you started screaming and got sick. What do you expect me to do when you're puking all over my shoes?"

Teknon interrupted the argument. "Guys!" he said, "can't you see your father is hurt?" The boys looked at their father's head but didn't respond. Teknon continued, "He was knocked unconscious and almost fell overboard."

noticed that the unconscious man had slipped toward the side of the boat and was about to fall overboard. Teknon shouted to his father, but Kratos couldn't hear him.

With his eyes fixed on the passenger, Teknon planted his feet as firmly as possible on the deck. Gauging his balance, he released his grip on the pole and leaned toward the man. When the next wave hit, Teknon almost lost his footing, but he struggled to within arm's reach of the man. Then Teknon recognized him. It was Pikros and Parakoe's father. *Where were his sons? Had they gone overboard in the storm?* Teknon wondered. Blood gushed from a wound on the man's head.

Teknon wrapped his arm around a nearby railing as tightly as possible and stretched to reach the man. In one last, desperate reach, Teknon grabbed the man by the back of his shirt and pulled as hard as he could to roll him back onto the deck. He then grabbed him under the arms, leaned back, and stumbled into the laundry room. After closing the door, Teknon looked at the man to make sure he was breathing. Then he grabbed a clean towel and held it tightly against the wound. Once the bleeding was under control, Teknon sat down by the man and waited.

An hour later, the Hudor Sea calmed and once again resembled glass. The sky cleared as fast as it had clouded, and passengers cautiously poked their heads from the lower decks. Three exhausted warriors met at the bow and slapped each other on the back.

"Well, I guess we all know that storm was no meteorological mishap," Kratos said, sitting down. "Magos must be using the precipitation technology he and I created on Basileia. We hoped to influence the weather in order to increase the output of crops."

"I think my arms are going to fall off," Tor said, sitting down and closing his eyes. "At least I know these braces work as I hoped they would. Hard to create a simulation like that back at the lab."

"You've got that right, big guy," Matty responded. "Outside of a few leaks and some squishy socks, I'd say these shoes performed to perfection."

After a few seconds of silence, Parakoe just said, "I'm hungry," and hit his older brother on the shoulder. "You said there would be something to eat." With that, the brothers walked away, continuing to bicker. Ameleo watched them and shook his head.

"I'm sorry," he said to the others. "I try to give them everything they want. I give them freedom to do what they wish. I just don't understand why they don't respect me." He struggled to his feet. Teknon tried to help him again, but he graciously refused. "I owe you a lot, young man," he said to Teknon. "I hope one day I can repay the debt." He shook hands with Teknon, then with the others, and followed after his sons.

Tor crossed his arms in disgust. "Sounds like discipline has been in short supply around Ameleo's house," he said.

"I can't believe how those two treat each other," Teknon said. "They constantly criticize and cut each other to pieces. How can they live like that?"

"Life is difficult when there's no respect for others, especially family," Kratos said, looking at his son. Teknon cringed. Kratos continued. "No matter what we accomplish, or who we impress, if we don't treat our family and friends with respect, we have nothing to offer. That's why I've never allowed you to show disrespect to your mother. It's all about honor. We must show honor to each other."

"Thinking of someone in particular, Dad?" Teknon said sheepishly.

Kratos smiled. "There's a little girl at home who thinks that you hung the second moon of Basileia. But all she gets from her big brother is criticism or the silent treatment. Why?"

"Because she acts like ... "

"Like a little girl," Matty finished, putting his finger to his temple. "Hmm, gee, I don't get it. Like a little girl, huh? Hey, maybe it's because she is a ... "

"Okay, I get it." Teknon scratched his head and looked toward the calm sea. "I guess I could be nicer to Hilly. I sure don't want us to end up like those guys."

"Treat her well, and you'll have a friend for life," Matty said. "Besides, you can choose your friends," he joked, "but you're stuck with your relatives."

"Not these friends," Tor bellowed with a laugh. "You're stuck with us, too."

"Speaking of sticky," Matty said, "I don't know about you guys, but I'm feeling ripe after that storm. Let's hit the showers."

Not everyone headed for the showers. A solitary deck steward was cleaning up at a nearby table, watching the team of warriors walk away. He projected an image back to headquarters, where an imposing, bionic figure sat watching.

"So," Magos said with metallic resonance from his bionic vocal cords, "my old partner is more powerful than I anticipated." He turned away from the screen. "No matter. His time will come." With that, the cyborg sat back in his massive chair and began developing his next attack.

An Excellent Choice

The *Ergonaut* docked in the city of Sarkinos, at the southern tip of Tarasso, during the early evening hours of the second day of the voyage. The team came ashore as night began to fall on what appeared to be a peaceful little village. Stores had closed, and vendors were locking their doors. A few people walked the streets, apparently returning home from a day's work. At first glance, Sarkinos seemed a strange location for a luxury cruise ship like the *Ergonaut* to use as a shuttle port.

But Kratos and his companions knew otherwise. Sarkinos was better known throughout out quadrant for its underground casinos and sensual holographic salons. The team watched as passengers from the *Ergonaut* hurried toward the middle of town. There, like a solitary monument, stood an enormous transparent elevator. The elaborately ornamented, crystalline fixture stood alone, with its doors open. Red light flooded the elevator's interior, eerily encasing everyone who entered.

A holograph of an attractive, well-dressed female appeared on the elevator's outer wall. She spoke in a sultry and tempting voice, "Walk this way. Hurry now! This is the way to your holiday of entertainment and fantasy. Come, tonight is your lucky night."

The passengers increased their pace as they heard the woman's invitation. Tor looked at the anxious crowd with contempt. "Dolts!" he brooded. "Look at them. Like sheepalopes running to the slaughter." The big fellow crossed his arms. "I wish we didn't have to follow them down into that hole. Kratos, are you sure your informant is staying here in Sarkinos?"

"That's where he said to meet him," Kratos replied, shaking his head in disbelief as the passengers squeezed themselves into the elevator that dropped quickly to the lower levels. "I don't like it any more than you do." He paused for a moment while gazing at the serene landscape of downtown Upper Sarkinos. "Strange place, Sarkinos," he continued. "So peaceful on the surface, yet corrupt and evil underneath."

"Well, let's get on with it," Matty said. "The sooner we find the informer, the sooner we hit the trail. Are you sure we really need this info, Kratos?"

"We've got to get updated intelligence on Magos' headquarters. We've tried to prepare as much as possible, but we want to avoid as many surprises as we can."

Teknon looked anxious. "I've heard about this place. Don't they have a lot of those imaging salons where they ... "

"Yep!" Tor said turning and looking straight at the lad. "And you're not getting within a hundred meters of them, kid."

Teknon smiled at his mentor.

"Well, gents," Matty said as he started to walk, "we've got an aquarium to ride."

The four looked up at the simulated woman on the elevator's internal monitor as the clear doors closed in front of them. Down they went. What seemed a millisecond later, the doors reopened to Lower Sarkinos, otherwise known as the Sarkinos Underground. Gone were the small shops and peaceful pedestrians of the surface. Music, bright lights, and constant invitations to enjoy various forms of amusement engulfed the team.

Teknon watched with intrigue as people laughed and shouted on their way into the gambling casinos. He also noticed that the nightclubs on the far end of the street looked different from the ones where he stood. There were more video screens on the walls, and most of the lights glowed in a reddish color.

"Here's our lodge," Kratos said, pointing ahead. "Let's go in and get settled. Then we can search for our informant."

Jungle Island, as the lodge was named, displayed a lively tropical theme throughout the facility. This motif included robotic animals swinging from the ceilings, holographs of waterfalls, and native uniforms worn by all employees. Kratos had reserved a suite large enough for the entire team. The rooms were spacious and included all of the elaborate extras common to guest rooms in Sarkinos. Matty took one look at a large, air-cushioned hammock on the veranda and immediately dropped on it with his hands behind his head. "Are you sure we shouldn't spend a few hours here talking over strategy?" Matty pleaded with a relaxed smile.

"Get up, Speedster," Tor said as he manipulated the controls on Matty's hammock. The air pressure bounced Matty up and down.

"Hey, watch it!" Matty cautioned, trying to regain his previous position.

Kratos noticed Teknon gazing out the window at the bright lights in the street. Suddenly Kratos decided to change the plan.

"Matty, you stay here with Teknon," Kratos said.

Teknon spun around. "What?!" he blurted out. "Aren't you going to take us?" He pointed to Matty, who was starting to doze off.

Kratos continued. "Tor and I will scope out the area. If we find who we're looking for, we'll bring him back to the lodge and call you in the room."

Teknon again looked out of the window, disappointed.

"Don't worry," Kratos said. "You won't miss any of the action. But we need to keep a low profile. I don't want to appear too conspicuous. You and Matty rest up, and we'll be back soon. Understood?"

"I guess," Teknon muttered.

"Take care," Matty said, his eyes barely open. He fell happily asleep before Tor and Kratos were out the door.

Teknon couldn't sleep a wink. He looked at the clock every few minutes, rolling from side to side as the hours crept by. Matty, on the other hand, slept so soundly that he didn't even stir when simulated fireworks exploded outside the lodge in a midnight celebration. Tired of gazing at the dark ceiling, Teknon got out of his bed and walked over to the voice-activated beverage dispenser to get a drink. He placed a goblet under the golden faucet. "Warm florne," he whispered, so as not to stir Matty. A thick, white, aromatic liquid immediately streamed into Teknon's glass. Teknon passed the glass under his nose to take in the sweet fragrance, then took a sip. The substance made its delicious journey through his throat and into his stomach. As he raised the goblet for another taste, Teknon turned toward the large window that allowed a view of the casino below. His eyes roamed back and forth across the floor where every cubic meter was covered with some type of entertaining activity.

Teknon turned to see his mentor enjoying his semi-comatose state, then looked back at the casino. *Why not take a walk around the casino lobby?* he thought. *I'll be back before Matty even opens his eyes.* Teknon put his unfinished drink on a table and started for the door. He passed his hand over the illuminated door-release sensor, and he cringed as the simulated cry of a hodgebeast rose from speakers on either side of the door.

"They think of everything in this place," Teknon grumbled as he glanced once more at Matty to make sure the "call of the jungle" hadn't awakened his friend.

Teknon was fascinated at the spectacle of so many people handing over money at the various gambling stations. He watched as a robotic dealer flipped pyramid-shaped dice to several people playing a game called Ten High. Teknon chuckled as the dealer announced in a metallic tone, "House wins this hand!" *No kidding*, Teknon thought.

Teknon spotted a familiar individual across the room. It was one of the passengers from the *Ergonaut* whispering to a large figure in a uniform. Teknon remembered talking casually with the man, telling him about the team's trip thus far. *What was his name?* Teknon thought. *Feuds? No ... Pseudes. Yeah, Mr. Pseudes, that's it.*

The tall, uniformed individual was human in form and powerful looking. *Probably an android*, Teknon thought. Teknon's interest increased and he weaved his way through the crowd without the two noticing him. The youth crouched behind a large, artificial plant and tried to listen to the conversation.

"I tell you they're looking for someone," Pseudes said to his tall companion. "You should have seen them during that storm your master created. If you're going to stop them, you'd better do it soon."

Teknon watched as the android nodded. Just then a cheer burst forth from a nearby table, as someone won a hand of Ten High. Teknon strained to hear more of the conversation, but couldn't. As the cheering subsided, Teknon watched as Pseudes and his confederate parted company. The android went to the back of the casino; Pseudes quickly left Jungle Island and proceeded down the street.

Teknon hesitated for a moment, then reached for a house phone to call Matty. *Matty probably won't even hear the beep,* he thought. *If I don't follow this guy now, we'll lose him. I've got to find out what they were talking about. I just need to keep up with him until Dad gets back.* Teknon peeked outside the front door of the lodge and spotted Pseudes, heading into the peculiar red region that Teknon had noticed before. Teknon, still trying to remain unnoticed, followed Pseudes and watched him enter a nightclub. As Teknon closed in, he felt a cold hand on his shoulder. Startled, he spun around, ready to strike whomever or whatever it was.

"Hello, my friend," said the good-looking, well-dressed gentleman. "Thinking of going in?"

Teknon, still shaken, babbled, "What? What do you mean? Go in where?"

"Why into the House of a Thousand Scenes, of course," the man said, pointing to the establishment behind Teknon.

Teknon turned around. "My name is Eros, and I'm the host of this pleasure palace. Please come in and sample our incredible selection of female holographs—all beautiful and all available for your viewing pleasure. You look like a fellow who would enjoy some manly entertainment like that."

Teknon tried to regain his wits, but felt very strange and uncomfortable.

"Why don't you come in tonight as our guest?" Eros continued. "If you like what you see, come back tomorrow night and bring your friends. What do you say?" Eros took Teknon gently by the arm and started leading him in. As they entered the club, Teknon noticed various images surrounding him. They were scenes of women doing things he knew he should not see.

Teknon tried to leave, but Eros tightened his grip, pulling the youth further into the maze of video screens and imaging rooms. Teknon was temporarily distracted by the bright lights and silhouettes of bodies beginning to materialize in front of him. When the images came into focus, he immediately turned his gaze away and wrenched his arm from Eros. Then he rushed out the door.

When Teknon got outside, he whipped around to scold Eros, only to find that the beckoning host had disappeared. Teknon's heart was racing. He was angry, scared, and relieved all at the same time. He didn't know what to do next, but he was happy to be out of that place.

Suddenly Teknon felt not one, but two distinctly different hands on his shoulder. He spun around again, this time to greet two familiar faces.

"Bit out of place, aren't we, lad?" Arti said with a smile.

"Arti!" Teknon exclaimed, then turned to the second individual. "Epps!" He grabbed both of them at the same time. "I don't know if I've ever been more glad to see anyone."

Epps, wearing his custom-made gloves, put his hand on Teknon's shoulder. "Glad to see you, too, pal," Epps said. "We saw what went on there a minute ago. Well done!"

"What do you mean?" Teknon asked.

Arti glanced around the corner and interrupted. "Enough of that for now," he said calmly. He pointed to the back door of the club. "It looks like our target is exiting by an alternate route." Pseudes, looking around to make sure no one was watching, started walking down a side street on his way to another club. Teknon and his friends started to follow. Pseudes accidentally dropped the bottle of gleukos he was carrying. As he stooped to pick it up, he noticed the three following him. He stood up quickly and began to run.

"Grab him, Arti!" Epps shouted.

Arti responded without hesitation by shooting a focused beam of energy from his face brace at the fleeing snitch. The bright yellow beam hit Pseudes squarely in the back and completely surrounded him. He froze, fixed in a running pose.

"Nice shot," Epps said.

"Of course," Arti responded, releasing his captive from the beam. Pseudes fell to the ground, stunned. The three companions helped the dazed stranger, now appearing as if he had consumed too much gluekos, back to their suite at the lodge. Kratos and Tor had just returned and were questioning Matty on the whereabouts of Teknon.

"Epps and Arti!" Matty yelled. "I'm glad you finally decided to show up. And as for you, young dude," he said, pointing at Teknon, "the next time you decide to go on a midnight sightseeing tour, let me in on it."

Tor and Matty began catching up with the other two mentors, while Kratos walked over to his son. "You had me worried," Kratos said. "Are you all right?" Teknon nodded. Kratos turned toward the subdued Pseudes. "And who do we have here?" he asked. "I see that he and Arti have already become acquainted."

"His name is Pseudes," Teknon said. "I heard him talking to what looked like an android dressed in a uniform down in the casino. They were talking about us. He described how we got through the storm and told the android that he'd better 'take care' of us now."

Kratos glanced at the mentors, who nodded with an understanding look. "You were right, Teknon," Kratos said. "That was an android." Pseudes rubbed his head and tried to focus his eyes.

Tor went over and picked up the man by his lapels. Pseudes' shoes left the ground. "We need some information, little man," the warrior growled.

Pseudes, still groggy, shook his head and yelled back, "Not a chance, you oversized lead-lummox!" Pseudes grunted, teeth clenched. Tor's face got tighter. The big warrior shoved Pseudes into a chair in the middle of the room, and towered in front of the squirming man.

"Well," Matty said, leaning against the wall, "this fellow's either got a great sense of humor or he's a raving lunatic. No one in their right mind would talk that way to Tor."

Kratos stepped in. "Epps, your assistance if you please."

"My pleasure," Epps responded as he walked behind Pseudes' chair and placed his hands gently on the man's shoulders. His gloves began to glow, pulsating with light.

Pseudes eyes became fixed in a pleasant expression. Looking past Tor into the distance, Pseudes was relaxed, and he smiled. After a few more moments of empty stares, he turned toward the group. "My, it's so good to see you all," he said. "I'm sorry I caused such a commotion back there in the street." He wobbled a bit and grinned at Tor. "It was in the street, wasn't it?"

Teknon, seeing the effect of Epp's gloves for the first time, began to laugh. "It's good to see you too, Mr. Pseudes," Teknon said, still chuckling as he walked over to Matty.

"My buddy, Epps," Matty said, "has got the touch!" Epps smiled in satisfaction.

Kratos began questioning Pseudes. "Mr. Pseudes, we understand that Magos has android soldiers around the area. Is that true?"

Pseudes nodded. "He has several types, you know."

"What are these soldiers like, and what abilities do they have?" Kratos continued.

"Well," Pseudes said willingly, "he has two types. First, he has the footsoldiers. Hideous, hulking brutes, programmed primarily to protect and fight. They are extremely strong. And they have an ability to blend in with their surroundings, I think, by using some sort of holographic device. They can

also communicate without speaking." Pseudes stopped momentarily to breathe a sigh of contentment.

Arti asked the next question. "How many footsoldiers does Magos have?"

"Oh, about 3000. They're all over the countryside, many of them surrounding his headquarters."

"Where is his headquarters?" Arti pressed.

"Northwest of here in the mountain region," Pseudes said. "You can't miss it. It's a massive structure. There's an entire battalion of androids guarding the perimeter."

"What's the headquarters like on the inside?" Tor asked.

"I don't know," Pseudes responded. "I've only seen it from a distance. I'm just an informant, you know. I make my living that way."

"And the other type of android?" Tor asked.

"Ah yes, the kakos," Pseudes replied, his face turning sour.

"Tell us about the kakos," Arti said.

"They are Magos' elite force. He only made 100 of them. The kakos are calculating, cruel, and deadly."

"Like Scandalon," Teknon whispered to Epps.

"They have the ability to change their shape into any form they desire," Pseudes continued.

Tor glanced at Kratos. "That much we knew."

"They also have advanced weaponry built into their structure. I don't know all that they can do, but I know they're extremely powerful."

Kratos paced slowly, stroking his beard, then running his hand through his hair. He motioned to Tor. "All right, Mr. Pseudes," Kratos said to the smiling man, "Our friend Tor will take you back to your room, where you can get a good night's sleep. But first, Epps would like to shake your hand." Kratos leaned over and whispered to Epps, "Give him enough to last at least 24 hours."

Epps nodded. "It was a pleasure to meet you, Mr. Pseudes," Epps said, his glove glowing as he shook Pseudes' hand. "Sleep well."

"Thank you," Pseudes said, smiling broadly. Tor took him by the arm and led him out of the room. After a few chuckles among the group, Kratos asked Arti and Epps about the evening.

"You would have been proud of him," Epps said, pointing to Teknon, who looked back with a puzzled expression.

Arti agreed. "Indeed. When we got to the scene, we saw someone trying to pull Teknon into an image salon. But Teknon came out immediately."

Tor, reentering the room, heard Arti's comment. "Tremendous!" Tor exclaimed, as he grabbed Teknon and tossed him into the air. Teknon landed firmly on his feet, but he still looked confused.

"What's the big deal?" he asked. "Arti and Epps are the ones who came to the rescue."

Matty walked over and put his hand on Teknon's shoulder. "Tek, it's not only what you did, but what you didn't do."

"You see, Teknon," Kratos added, "you had the opportunity, with none of us around, to make a bad choice by exposing yourself to images that could have warped your perspective."

"On what?" Teknon asked.

"On the gift of intimacy. Those types of pictures can be pleasurable and tempting, but they give a distorted view of women and love. Once you see those images, it's difficult to forget them. Those places degrade women. And once you get into the habit of viewing that kind of material, you can get hooked and you will eventually damage your character. To become a CHAMPION, we must each exercise purity in our minds as well as our bodies."

"It's not easy to stay pure in a hole like the Sarkinos Underground," Tor snarled. "This place is crawling with imaging salons. It would've been better if you'd stayed in your room in the first place."

"You're probably right," Teknon said.

"Tor *is* right," Epps said. "You took a big chance when you decided to go out on your own and walk past those places. All of us are tempted to look at bad material like that, but we can't afford to take those kinds of risks. We've got to stay as far away from them as possible."

"You're right, I blew it," Teknon said with a sigh. Then looking to his dad he said, "I should have trusted your instincts."

"This kind of temptation is more dangerous than you can imagine because once we sample that trash," Kratos added, "it becomes part of us and lives in us. Every day we have to make the right choices. You shouldn't have been near that salon in the first place. Tonight, though, when you had the opportunity, you chose not to look. You made an excellent choice."

"And we also got Pseudes to squeal," Matty said, reclining on the cushion of air. "Not a bad night! Y'know, now that Arti and Epps are here, I must say that I pity the goons that Magos puts in our path."

"Well," Kratos said, "we didn't find *our* informant. Maybe he'll show up later. But we didn't come away empty-handed, either." Kratos smiled. "What do you say we go downstairs and treat ourselves to one of those massive Sarkinos desserts? I still can't get over how inexpensive the food is around here."

"If you spent as much money as these gamblers, they'd probably pay you to eat the food," Tor said. "I say we go downstairs and celebrate our young warrior's good sense."

The team made its way down through the casino and into the Safari Café, which was complete with exotic holographic animals, which appeared to wander among the customers while they ate. As Teknon polished off his dessert, he watched his teammates eating, talking, and enjoying themselves. He was struck with the fact that, just a short time earlier, he had been faced with a temptation that could have caused him trouble and frustration if he had yielded. He smiled to himself and thought, *I'm glad I made the right choice.*

EPISODE EIGHT

FACED WITH FEAR

The night air was cool and damp as the team walked down a boggy trail outside of Sarkinos. Rain fell hard, but lasted less than an hour. It was just enough to make the ground soft and walking more difficult than normal.

Matty looked at his fancy footwear in disgust. "Look at this. The mud is all over these things. How am I supposed to keep up my flawless image with muddy wheels?"

Epps laughed. "Nothing like a little muck to help bring you down to earth, eh Mat?" Matty grinned as he pulled his foot from another puddle of slush.

"Where are we going?" Teknon inquired, pushing through the mud.

"To a small mining village," Kratos replied. "I think our slippery informant may be there."

"And why would you think that?" Teknon asked.

"Just trust me on this one, Teknon. I have a little history with our informant."

As they entered a clearing in the woods, Kratos held up his hand for the group to stop and take a short rest. Epps, Matty, and Teknon sat down. Arti, glancing at his hand-held Sensatron, spoke up. "The village is two kilometers northwest. We should reach it within the hour."

"Well, I hope your timid contact makes an appearance," murmured Tor as he pulled an energy bar from his pocket. "Especially after standing us up in Sarkinos."

Kratos turned around. "We don't know that, Tor. He may have met with some difficulty that prevented him from keeping his appointment with us. Besides, a small, obscure village might be a better place to talk."

Suddenly a light on the Sensatron began to flash. Arti stood up. His eyes narrowed. He turned his head from side to side, looking in different directions.

Kratos noticed Arti's uneasiness and asked, "What's up, Arti?"

"Something's not right," he said in a low tone as he looked quickly in the opposite direction. "Not right at all, Kratos."

Kratos spoke quickly in the same low tone. "Arti, quick, scan the area." Tor, sensing the tension, braced himself. Matty stood up.

Arti's brow wrinkled and his eyes narrowed. A bright, white beam shot out from his face band. At first the beam was sharp and focused, then it widened. Arti began covering the perimeter, while all eyes fixed on the beam. Teknon stumbled a bit as he stood up. Arti's beam had only covered a third of the clearing when, in the light, there appeared the outline of large ominous forms.

"Footsoldiers!" Kratos yelled. "Warriors—back to back!"

The team members responded like a knee hit with a reflex hammer. In a split second, they formed a circle, all facing outward and ready for battle. Teknon, dazed, stood in the middle of the formation. Suddenly, hazy outlines began to materialize around the clearing. Hulking beings, larger even than Tor, moved closer to the team. "There's 10 of them!" Teknon hollered. Then he pointed in another direction. "No, there's five more!"

Tor, displaying his typical bravado, shouted to the rest as he leaped forward, "Let's roll 'em!" The hulking mentor's foot landed squarely on the chest of the leading footsoldier, pushing him back into two other androids. Another footsoldier planted a forceful backhand across Tor's head. He stumbled, then recovered quickly.

Arti shot his stun beam at an oncoming footsoldier, who barely slowed. He dodged the swing of the footsoldier's mechanized hand with ease. A small door slid open on the androids's chest and a metallic cable shot like a lightning bolt in Arti's direction. It wrapped around Arti's leg, pulling the warrior onto his back with a thud. As the android raised a fist to strike, Arti used his free leg to crack the knee of his opponent. The footsoldier doubled over. Arti braced his arms, lifting himself off the ground. At the same time, he delivered a kick across the soldier's face. The cable released, and the footsoldier splashed down hard into the mud.

Matty ran in and out between three of the androids, stunning them with strikes to the face and abdomen. One of them swung his fist in Matty's direction, only to miss the warrior and hit another footsoldier. Matty laughed to himself as he zipped around to make another pass. Becoming overconfident, he slowed down just enough for a footsoldier to see him and hold out an immense arm as a barrier. The android clotheslined Matty, knocking the speedster off his feet. Matty, dazed, shook his head and focused his eyes only to see two footsoldiers preparing to attack.

Epps swooped over Matty, kicking one, and then another footsoldier across their chins. Epps landed gracefully on his feet in his fighting stance. Another android shot a cable in Epps' direction. Matty, fully recovered, intercepted the cable in mid-flight, and wrapped it around three more of the footsoldiers. Static energy erupted from all three and their circuits shorted out.

Teknon watched the fighting from an increasing distance. Bewildered by his indecision as to what he should do next, he looked quickly in one direction, then the other. *Should I join the team and fight?* he wondered. Torn by confusion and fear, he crouched low and watched Tor as the big man wrapped his retention beam around five footsoldiers, raising them up and down like a ball on a wire. Teknon ran and hid behind a large rock.

Teknon didn't notice the form lurking behind him, poised to slam its powerful fists down to crush the boy. The youth turned just in time to see the forceful blow become absorbed by a force field only half a meter from his head. Before the footsoldier could recoil, the surgical impact of the Hoplon severed his mechanical head. The shield returned to Kratos as sparks flew from the frazzled wires of the android's frame.

But relief quickly turned to horror as Teknon watched a telescoping cable slither from behind his father, and wrap around his body before the Hoplon could reach his hand. Kratos' face grimaced in pain as the cable began to tighten. Teknon stood up to run to Kratos as he saw the shield bounce off the coil of the cable and fall to the ground.

Just then a focused energy beam hit Kratos' captor in the back. The cable did not release, but the footsoldier was thrown off balance. Tor's huge fist swung as if shot from a cannon. It connected with the soldier's chin, and hurled the android backward. Tor used his other hand to grasp the cable so that Kratos would not be pulled along; then the massive warrior snapped the cable in two. It released and Kratos fell to one knee, tightly holding his side. Matty sped to Kratos and helped him to his feet.

Some of the footsoldiers lay in pieces around the clearing. The others had vanished when all hope of victory was gone.

"You all right, Captain?" Matty asked, concern in his eyes.

"I think a few of my ribs are broken." Kratos looked anxiously over toward Teknon and saw his son rise slowly from behind a rock. "Teknon! You're all right! Come here."

Teknon responded slowly and reluctantly. His heart still pounded with fear from the battle. But now he felt another sensation that bothered him much more. He felt embarrassed. He felt like a failure.

"Dad, how bad is it?" Teknon dropped to his father's side.

Tor chuckled to break the tension. "Not enough to slow him down."

Epps finally returned from his battle. He stopped in

front of Kratos and looked intently at the way the leader held his chest.

"Can you fix him up, Epps?" Matty asked.

"No problem," Epps replied as he walked to his leader's side. "Now Kratos," Epps said, "just relax." He placed his hands on either side of Kratos' ribcage. "This is going to feel a bit strange." The alloy of his gloves began to shine, and Kratos closed his eyes with a look of satisfaction. After a few moments, Epps released him. Kratos continued to breathe deeply as his mental focus returned. He pressed his hand against his chest. The pain was gone. He looked at Epps with admiration.

"Amazing, Epps," he said to his gloved companion. Epps smiled and stepped back. Kratos picked up the Hoplon and placed it into the harness. "Well," he continued as he looked around the clearing, "not a bad showing for our first encounter with Magos' footsoldiers."

"I'll say," Matty replied. "And I was just getting warmed up. I wonder when Magos is going to send in the first-string?"

Teknon, his shoulders slightly bowed and head lowered, spoke to his father, "Why didn't you flatten that footsoldier when he grabbed you?"

Kratos looked back at his son and smiled. "Because I was protecting you," he replied.

"But couldn't you do both at once?" Teknon continued.

"No, unfortunately I can only use one feature of the Hoplon at a time. If I choose to use the force field, I can't utilize the increased strength it can give me."

Teknon turned and faced the opposite direction so that his father could not see the pained expression on his face. He used his arm to lean against a rock. "So by helping me, you left yourself open to attack."

"It was an easy choice to make, Teknon," Kratos responded. "You're my son."

"And my team member, kid," Tor chimed in, grabbing Teknon by the shoulder. "I'd have done the same thing."

"I got confused," Teknon said, facing into the distance. "I ran away. I thought I was ready to fight when the time came." Teknon's eyes started to water. "And I put Dad in danger when he protected me."

"It takes time to learn how to respond correctly in battle," Epps said, trying to comfort Teknon. "Don't cut yourself down for pulling back today. You learn by doing."

Matty stepped in. "That's a fact Teknon," the speedster said confidently. "You know, I remember one time, back in the Mache Region, when we were surrounded by ... "

"Yes, Matty," Arti interrupted, his mouth curling in a smile, "I think we recall that incident quite well. Now, shouldn't we resume our hike to the mining village?"

"Right," Kratos agreed. "Let's get going. We need to get there by nightfall." As the team continued walking on the wet path, Kratos noticed a small pack he had neglected to pick up after the battle. "Teknon, would you grab that hip-pack for me?" Teknon nodded and proceeded toward the other side of the clearing.

No one noticed a figure slowly emerging from behind a cluster of trees. It was an android more refined than the bulky footsoldiers, one with a body that shined and glimmered in the moonlight. This particular android had been sent when it became apparent that the footsoldiers were losing the battle. He slowly raised a weapon to his shoulder, and aimed directly at the warriors. This android was familiar to the group, although they would not have recognized him. Scandalon was now in his true manifestation as one of Magos' kakos. From the shadows, he squeezed the firing mechanism on the weapon. A piercing sound rang out and a powerful, bright beam shot directly at the team. Teknon, out of the line of fire, turned quickly when he heard the high whining pitch of the beam leaving the gun.

Although Kratos and his comrades also heard the sound, they could not react in time. Teknon watched helplessly as the beam surrounded the five men, encasing them in what looked like a crystalline dome.

With the dome now complete, Scandalon stopped shooting and slipped away into the night. Once the brightness of the beam subsided, the warriors were enveloped by some sort of containment field, three meters wide and four meters high. It glowed and pulsated with a dull fluorescence. Arti, gaining his composure, immediately pulled out his diagnostic instrument. Teknon ran to the edge of the field and started to touch it. "No, Teknon, don't touch it!" Arti screamed. "It's made of tantronic energy. One touch, and you'll disintegrate!" Teknon stepped back quickly, but not far.

"Is it solid energy, Arti?" Kratos asked.

"Yes," Arti replied, "so solid we can't penetrate it." He continued to look at the small screen. His frown intensified. "And that's not all."

"There's more?" Matty inquired.

"The field is shrinking!" Arti said. "In two hours, it will engulf us."

Kratos scanned and analyzed the tantronic field, then barked an order. "All right, here's what we're going to do. Tor and Arti, when I give the word, focus your beams in a wide array on the roof of the field. I'll do the same with my force field. Let's see if we can lift this thing off the ground." Arti and Tor nodded. Kratos continued. "On my count ... one ... two ... three!"

Light again filled the area. Tor's arm braces lit up as he clenched his fists and concentrated on lifting the field. Arti did the same, shooting a wide beam of energy across the roof. Kratos sent an invisible force wave to combine with the other attempts. The three warriors pushed with intense strain and effort, but to no avail. Soon, Kratos motioned to cease their efforts.

Exhausted, Kratos spoke to Arti. "Did we at least slow the shrinkage?" He asked, breathing heavily.

"Negative."

"Okay," Matty said, arms crossed, "what's plan B?"

Kratos dropped down to one knee. Teknon, still silent, watched his father and companions work through this tense situation. He was amazed at their calmness and lack of anxiety as they talked over the available options. Suddenly Kratos looked directly at Teknon. Kratos stepped as close to the edge of the field as possible and spoke to his son. "I've got an idea," he said, "and it's all up to you."

"Me?" Teknon said, stunned.

"It's our only hope, and you're the only one who can do it."

Teknon's arm dropped to his side. His body froze. He opened his mouth as if to respond, but his mouth went dry and he couldn't find the words. Teknon had no idea what his dad was about to say, but already his heart started pounding. *What can I possibly do?* he thought to himself.

EPISODE NINE

RECOVER, RECOVER, RECOVER

"Tell me this isn't happening," Teknon murmured to himself. His father's words replayed over and over through his mind. *What does Dad mean, it's up to me?* Even though Teknon's mind was racing, everything else seemed to be moving in slow motion. His palms were starting to sweat and he found it hard to focus his thoughts.

"Teknon! Did you hear me?" Kratos said, raising his voice. His speech was thick and garbled with static as it filtered through the tantronic energy field. Teknon fought to clear his mind.

"Wha ... what?" He tried to reply. "Yeah, Dad, I heard you." Teknon walked closer to the field. "What do you mean it depends on me? What can *I* do?"

"A group of mining families called the Phaskos live in the village ahead. They sustain themselves through mining and selling a substance called mamonas. In order to separate the mamonas from the walls of the mine shaft, the Phaskos use a powerful tool called a Lacerlazer, which will cut through tantronic energy." Kratos paused for a moment and motioned with his hands for emphasis. "Teknon, you've got to go to the village and convince the Phaskos to bring the Lacerlazer up here and cut through this field." Teknon's eyes widened, and he started to open his mouth.

Kratos began to talk faster. "I know you probably don't like the idea, but it's our only option at this point. And you're the only one who can do it. I know you can do it!"

Teknon looked from side to side and paused for a moment then replied, "Dad, I can't convince people I don't know to bring their cutter up here. There's got to be another way. Get Tor and Arti to try their beams again."

Arti looked at the Sensatron. "The field has receded another 30 centimeters!"

"Teknon," Kratos said firmly, "you've got to go, and you've got to go now." Kratos turned to his swift companion. "Matty, coach Teknon quickly on how to persuade the Phaskos." Matty nodded.

"Tek," Matty said, "since the town is small, you'll need to find the local hangout. It's probably a diner or something. Go in there and look the people over before you speak. The Phaskos are a fairly timid clan. You've got to motivate them to help you. See if there's a leader in the bunch. If there is, go directly to the decision maker. If not, you'll have to get everyone's attention."

"But Matty," Teknon said, pointing at him, "you're the public speaker, not me. I'm not the salesman in this group; you are. How is a young stranger supposed to get anyone's attention?"

"Think on three things, Tek. First, walk in there with confidence and authority. Go through the doors with your head up, your shoulders back, and the look of a CHAMPION on your face. Step two, scan the room and try to see what's going on. Once you've introduced yourself, start asking questions. Is there a problem in the group? Do they have a need? Remember, you can't motivate someone if you can't meet a need. If you can identify a need, remember it. Third, state the problem simply. See what their reaction is. If they resist, keep asking questions about what their needs might be. See if you can bargain with them. Think clearly, and remember that these people thrive on encouragement."

"Now wait a minute," Teknon said. "What if I do all this, and they still don't understand? What if they just don't like me? What if ... "

Tor interrupted. "If you do it like Matty says, they will understand. And they'll respect your position. That's all that matters. Now listen, kid, in less than two hours there's going to be a fireworks show around here, with us as the fireworks. You can do this. Now get going!" Tor put his massive hands firmly on his hips. "And keep a sharp eye for footsoldiers."

Teknon's mouth dropped open.

"Teknon," Epps added, "appeal to their emotions. Feel for them, and they'll feel for you."

"The clock is running," Arti said. "You have exactly one hour and 45 minutes."

Teknon took a deep breath. He knew what he had to do. He had to put the footsoldier incident behind him and recover his courage. He tried to control his anxiety, while consciously changing his facial expression from one of fear to one of determination. "I'll be back," he said firmly, "with the men and the tool! Don't worry!" With that he turned and began running toward the village.

Teknon ran almost at full speed, guided by the moonlit path in front of him. He wasn't tired. Bolts of adrenaline, combined with hours of rigorous training on the simulator, gave him all of the stamina he needed to reach the village quickly. With his body on autopilot, Teknon began thinking about what he would say to the Phaskos. *How did Matty put it?* he pondered. *Be confident, observe the scene, find the need, and state the case.* Although still anxious, Teknon slowly began to replace his fear of failing with an increasing determination to complete his mission. *Dad and the guys think I can do this. I'm going to do it! I've got to do it!*

Then Teknon heard a strange noise. It sounded like softly spoken words carried past him by the wind. He looked around as he ran, but nothing appeared. He shook his head, and kept running. Then he heard it again; the voice was faint but clear. This time he understood the message.

"Teknon, what are you doing?" the voice asked. Teknon still didn't see anyone. He wondered if he was hearing things. Maybe they were his own thoughts. He couldn't worry about it, though. He had to keep running.

The voice continued, "Who are you trying to fool? Didn't you just fail with those footsoldiers? You don't actually think the Phaskos are going to listen to a young coward, do you? You don't stand a chance. There's got to be a better way." Teknon winced as the voice penetrated his ears. He closed his eyes momentarily, but he didn't stop running. He knew if he allowed the voice to dismantle his confidence, he would slow down enough to doubt and reconsider his plan. If he took time to seek another method to save his father and friends, he might be too late!

Teknon couldn't see his enemy running on a parallel path, matching his run step for step. Scandalon, using his holographic stealth capabilities to make himself invisible, had begun to transmit high-frequency messages to Teknon. Scandalon was being instructed by Magos, who was tuned into his servant's pursuit to stop the youth before he reached the village. But the kako was commanded to forgo immediate assassination and focus on deceiving Teknon and dissolving his confidence. Magos was sure he could convert the boy to his way of thinking. Scandalon continued to intensify his message. "You're not a CHAMPION. You're a failure. Remember how you ran away during the fight? How can you come back after that? You've got to stop and find another way. Stop now! Stop!"

Teknon fought the mounting urge to stop. The voice bothered him tremendously, but he knew he had to press on. *Just a few hundred meters*, he thought. He clenched his fists and increased his speed. "I don't care if a footsoldier jumps onto the path. He'll have to take me out to stop me!" Scandalon stopped at the edge of the village. Expressionless as usual, the cloaked android found a secluded place to wait for Teknon's return.

When Teknon reached the village, he paused to rest. Although breathing heavily, he did not sit or even crouch to regain his strength. He stood in the middle of the street with his hands on his hips, amazed at how small the village was. A handful of miniature houses crowded the one road going through town. A few compact hovercars lined the street; many huddled around a well-lit building with open doors. Inside, Teknon could see many individuals talking around a large table. As they talked, they ate.

"Matty was right," Teknon said aloud. "The local hangout!"

He hesitated for a moment before going in. "Shoulders back, with a look of confidence," he reminded himself. As he entered the small tavern he found himself in the middle of an enormous feast. A large, circular table filled much of the room's center, covered with containers brimming with bizarre foods of many types and varieties. Teknon noticed from the seamless texture of the table that it must have been cut from a single massive piece of stone. More than 20 of the most unusual creatures Teknon had ever seen crowded around the table. All were too busy stuffing their mouths with food to see the youth entering the room.

Teknon also noticed that most of the Phaskos stood half a meter shorter than he. Though small in stature, they all had stocky muscular frames. None of them had a hair on their heads, which, combined with the rest of their bodies, gave them a striking resemblance to the hump of a sabercamel. Three thick pointed fingers on each hand made it look as if dexterity would be difficult. A multi-jointed thumb, however, provided a tight grip as they held utensils and bowls.

Their eyeballs were coal black except for white pupils, which seemed to glow like pearls in a saucer of ink. Each Phasko wore a pair of shaded goggles loosely around their necks, which Teknon guessed they used to shield their eyes from the light of day. He also observed that, between mouthfuls, the Phaskos were carefully studying what looked like a detailed map of the area displayed on the wall. Much to Teknon's dismay, none of the Phaskos seemed to be taking leadership in the conversation. That meant only one thing.

Plan B, according to Matty, Teknon thought. *I guess it's time to make the pitch.* Teknon walked around the table, trying to find the most strategic position to speak. He stopped, turned around, and took a deep breath.

"Excuse me," Teknon said. None of the Phaskos turned to look. They heard nothing over the clatter of their conversation. Teknon tried again. "Hello!" he said, raising his voice slightly. No response.

"Hey!" Teknon yelled at the top of his lungs. All talking at the table stopped. Spoons halted on their way to the Phaskos' mouths. Suddenly all eyes at the table were on a young, trembling teenager. The abrupt silence was so overwhelming that Teknon temporarily lost his train of thought and his mouth went as dry as a stale piece of bread. He looked around the room, searching for the right word to start his speech.

A Phasko on the far side of the table, his mouth stuffed with food, rose to his feet. "Who are you, young one?" he said in a muffled tone as he pointed to Teknon, "What do you seek?"

"We need help, now!" Teknon blurted out.

"We?" another Phasko asked with a frown as he continued chewing.

"My father and friends. They're trapped in a clearing close by. They're surrounded by a tantronic energy field. It's closing in on them." Teknon glanced at his watch on the underside of his wrist. "I've got exactly 63 minutes to save them."

"Save them?" asked the standing Phasko. "How could we possibly help you to save them? How did they become surrounded by tantronic energy?"

"We're not quite sure what happened," replied Teknon. "One minute they were in the clear, the next, a beam of light surrounded them. My dad said you have some kind of tool, a laser that can cut through the field. You've got to help me!"

"Why weren't you captured?" the Phasko probed.

"I was separated from the team when the beam hit," Teknon explained. "I guess the attacker was satisfied when he saw my father and the others caught inside the field."

"Were you followed here?" another Phasko inquired.

"I'm not sure. I don't think so," Teknon responded.

The Phaskos glanced at each other with a look of mutual understanding.

"Did you see any large creatures around?" one of the Phaskos asked. "Powerful looking androids with the third arm that shoots out from their bodies?"

"Third arm?" Teknon asked. Then he caught on. "Oh, you mean the footsoldiers. Yeah, the ones with the cable that shoots from their chest. Yes, we fought about 15 of them. Why do you ask?"

"Did you defeat them?" the Phasko inquired.

"Yes we did," Teknon replied. Then he hesitated. "I mean, my father and my friends beat them."

The Phaskos were silent for a moment. The Phasko on the far side still stood as he spoke. "I'm sorry. It would take our entire group to carry the Lacerlazer to the clearing. We cannot spare all of them at the moment. I'm sorry for your loss." At that, the Phasko reluctantly sat down and resumed his feasting.

"Sorry for my loss?" Teknon said, blood beginning to swell through his neck and into his face. His expression revealed anger and frustration as he wondered, *What's my next move? How can these people eat, when five men's lives are at stake?* Remembering Matty's coaching, he determined that the Phasko who was standing might be the leader of the group. Also, it seemed that the Phaskos were familiar with the footsoldiers and obviously didn't like them. *That's something we have in common*, Teknon thought. *But they said they didn't have the men to spare. Why?*

Teknon looked again at the group. Everyone had resumed their vigorous eating, but they also continued to examine the map. Teknon decided to try another tactic. "If you don't mind me asking, why are you studying that map?" he asked as he approached the table.

The Phasko whom Teknon had identified as the leader responded. "Two of our young children wandered into the hills this afternoon. We haven't been able to find them. Night is falling and the temperature will soon begin to drop. The Feared One's creatures roam around these hills, especially at night, plus we've spotted amachos in the area. The little ones could be anywhere, and we've got to send out a search party."

Teknon's mind raced again. *Feared One?* he thought. *They must mean Magos.* Here was the need he was looking for. A smile came over his face, and he began to speak, this time with confidence.

"I have an idea," Teknon said. "My friends trapped in the tantronic field have incredible talents. One runs so fast you can barely see him. Another can heal wounds just by touching them. If you free them, I promise that the fast one will look over the entire countryside for your children. And if they're hurt, my friend Epps will treat their injuries. What do you say?"

The Phaskos again looked at each other. The leader motioned to the rest to huddle closer so they could talk. Teknon, looking again at the time, decided to become more aggressive.

"Look," he said, "in 55 minutes my father and friends will dissolve into thin air. When they're gone, so are your hopes of finding your children tonight. Are you with me, or aren't you?"

"We are!" stated the leader. "Anyone who fights the creatures of the Feared One is a friend of the Phaskos. We would greatly appreciate your friends' help in finding our young ones."

"Then let's get moving!" Teknon said enthusiastically. He turned quickly toward the door, then stopped. He realized he had not completed Matty's instructions.

"This is a great deed you're doing," Teknon said to group. "The Phaskos are a fine and courageous people." The Phaskos looked at Teknon, smiling with appreciation for the encouragement. *Right again, Matty*, Teknon thought.

As the Phaskos prepared to leave the room, Teknon noticed that each reached underneath the table and produced a pair of long brass-colored gloves. Each of the gloves was studded with large, ominous-looking spikes, which started at the shoulder and continued down over the knuckles. As the small miners fit their oversized hands inside the armored gloves, Teknon pointed at one of them and asked, "What are those for?"

"Digging, of course," the leader calmly responded.

In less than five minutes, 22 Phaskos were pushing a large, complex machine down the street. "Doesn't this thing have a propulsion unit to drive it along?" Teknon asked the leader. "Why do they have to push it?"

"The propulsion unit is broken at the moment," the leader replied.

Even with the large number of helpers, Teknon could not believe that the Phaskos could move the immense laser. *Strong little guys, aren't they?* he thought. The leader walked quickly with Teknon behind the laser.

"By the way," Teknon asked, "how could you guys eat like that when so much was going on? If it were me, I wouldn't have been able to think of food at a time like that."

"Eating calms our nerves," replied the Phasko. "When we're scared, we eat." Teknon glanced at the Phasko's stocky figure.

I guess these guys must worry a lot, Teknon thought. "By the way," Teknon said to his new companion, "what's your name?"

"Phileo," the stout fellow replied. "And yours?"

"Teknon," Teknon said, sticking out his hand. A thick, muscular hand returned. Both squeezed warmly.

The caravan of men and machine hurried up the trail to the clearing. The laser resembled a centipede as it traveled along, with the short, chunky legs of the Phaskos trotting along on either side. As Teknon and Phileo exchanged information, Teknon began hearing the strange voice again. This time it sounded more eager than before, and more threatening.

"You don't think these people like you, do you?" the voice stated. "They don't! Just because they said they would come along doesn't mean that they believe you or your pitiful pleading. How could they follow a cowardly failure like you? Soon they will realize who's leading them. Then they'll turn back, and it will be over!"

Teknon's attention diverted from Phileo as the youth strained to determine the source of the voice. Suddenly he stopped and listened carefully to the tormenting words.

Instead of trying to ignore the sounds, Teknon now studied them, analyzing the texture of the phrases as they continued to flow past his ears and into the night. He turned his head slowly in different directions as he began to hear a low hum accompanying the voice, resembling the static he often heard in communication devices. Teknon now recognized the voice for what it was: a fabricated message, probably relayed from a nearby remote location. His expression of determination intensified.

"What's the matter?" Phileo asked. Teknon motioned to Phileo to lower his voice and keep walking. Phileo also began looking around.

"Is there a path like this one nearby?" Teknon whispered. Phileo nodded, then pointed to the left, behind a row of trees. Teknon signaled for the group to keep walking.

"We don't seem to be making good time, do we?" Teknon said, raising his voice for emphasis. His expression told Phileo that he was about to do something.

Suddenly Teknon veered to the left, bounded through the trees and jumped on top of a large rock just short of the other path. There, slowing to a halt, was an extraordinary android. Scandalon stood motionless, looking at Teknon without expression or emotion. The android's smooth, sleek shape glistened in the moonlight, and almost seemed to shift and move within itself. Teknon felt as if he were looking at a man composed of liquid silver. Teknon knew that if he waited a second longer his enemy would use his holographic ability to blend into the background. Then he would be vulnerable to attack from the invisible foe. Teknon sprang and placed a powerful kick on the jaw of his opponent. Scandalon's head spun around as if it were a coin on a table.

The kako's head completed the circle and froze into position. His eyes now beamed bright red and focused on the young warrior. Scandalon's fingers shifted in size and shape to produce a razor-sharp blade that caught the light of the moon just enough to reveal its dangerous structure. He extended his hand and thrust it toward Teknon. The lower part of his fluid, mechanical arm lengthened and shot forward like a spear. Teknon dodged, but not before the blade caught him on the edge of his left forearm. He winced in pain as he rolled, coming up again in a fighting stance. Teknon quickly grabbed his wound and tried to slow the bleeding.

As he stood face-to-face with Scandalon, Teknon thought he actually saw a smile forming on the android's face. *I think he's enjoying this*, Teknon thought. The bladed arm retracted as Scandalon again pointed his hand toward Teknon, who prepared himself to dodge the next attack.

Without notice, the ground erupted underneath Scandalon, throwing him off balance. A whirling form appeared in the newly opened soil, and a small, bulky figure swung a huge fist that collided with Scandalon's jaw. The glistening android flew off his feet and slammed down on his back.

Teknon yelled in recognition. "Phileo!"

Before Teknon could say another word, the Phasko was above ground and on his feet. He turned to face Scandalon, who had regained his balance. Phileo's face revealed his intense hatred for the kako. Teknon watched as the chemical compounds in Phileo's body immediately started shifting in composition, almost as if from the molecular level. Phil's frame hardened, no longer resembling flesh and bone. His body turned into what seemed to Teknon to be solid rock. The Phasko crouched and looked as if he would attack Scandalon again.

Scandalon hesitated, then turned and darted in the opposite direction, Teknon watched as the android hastily engaged his holographic mode and disappeared.

Teknon, still grasping his wound, walked quickly to his helper. "How in the world?" he asked, bewildered.

"Later, my friend," Phileo said, grasping Teknon's good arm. "Now we must hurry to save your father."

Teknon and his new friends entered the clearing with only three minutes remaining. The youth gasped as he observed that the tantronic field had almost completely closed in on his father and mentors. They were all laying facedown, one on top of the other, with Tor closest to the field. The field was centimeters from Tor's back, and the big fellow strained not to move.

"We're here, Dad!" Teknon shouted. "Don't worry, we'll have you out in no time." He turned to Phileo. "We will, won't we?"

The Lacerlazer was already in position. Phileo barked an order to his team. "All right my brothers, anchor!"

Four Phaskos positioned themselves on each corner of the laser platform. Immediately they began spinning down, head first, like drills going into wood. Within seconds they had completely burrowed into the soil. Other Phaskos grabbed cables attached to the laser's platform and dropped them into the holes. Teknon watched as the laser was pulled tightly to the ground. Phileo moved quickly to the laser controls and programmed it for firing. He called to the captured men. "Stay very still, my friends."

"Just don't singe the hair," Matty's muffled voice came from underneath the pile.

"Fire!" Phileo commanded.

A bright, focused beam shot toward the tantronic energy field. Like a surgeon's knife, the laser sliced through the integrity of the dangerous substance until an opening was created large enough for the captives to escape. Soon all five men were free, and they could finally stand up and stretch.

"One minute and 33 seconds remaining," Arti said, sounding relieved.

"A bit too cozy for me, gents," Matty said, brushing himself off.

Teknon rushed to hug his father and said, "Dad, we've got to help these people. They have children lost in the countryside, and they're in danger. I told them that Matty could find the children, and that Epps could take care of them if they were hurt."

Matty responded instantly. "I'm off. Epps, I'll see you back in the village."

"If they're hurt, Matty, don't move them," Epps said. "Come and get me first." Matty nodded and zipped away.

Epps grabbed Phileo warmly on the arm. "I'll head to the village right away," Epps said, pointing to the rest of the Phaskos. "Should I take the rest of them with me?"

"Yes, thank you," replied Phileo.

"I'll join you, Epps," Arti said, putting the Sensatron on his belt. He nodded at Kratos and Teknon. "See you soon. Well done, Teknon."

"Yes, great job," Epps added. Arti joined him as they assisted the Phaskos in returning the laser. When the laser was out of sight, Kratos walked over to Phileo. The two embraced each other like long-lost brothers.

Teknon was puzzled by the scene. "What? Do you guys know each other?"

"From way back, Teknon," Kratos said, as he looked down and grasped the Phasko with both hands. "How long has it been, Phil?"

"Don't start talking about how far back we go, Kratos. Remember, Phaskos live longer than Basileians. You're much older than me as it is. I'll have to start calling you *old man!*"

Teknon rubbed his forehead. "All right, I've obviously missed the gag." He looked at his father. "What's going on here? When and how did you meet this guy?"

"I'll explain that later, Teknon," Kratos said, looking proudly at his son. "But for now, I think congratulations are due. You persuaded the Phaskos to bring the laser. Well done." Kratos looked over at Phil.

"How did he do, Phil?" Kratos asked.

"I think there's a CHAMPION somewhere in that young body, Kratos," Phil responded. "He performed admirably." Kratos smiled at Phil's comment.

"So Phileo is your informant?" Teknon asked. Kratos nodded. "But why didn't you tell me he was there? I thought I didn't have a friend in the world when I got to that village."

"He wanted you to think that," Phil interjected. "None of the other Phaskos know that your dad and I are friends. It might scare them to think that Magos is your father's archenemy. Your father didn't want to take any chances that you would reveal my secret."

"Besides," Kratos said, "you needed to break out of your comfort zone by persuading the Phaskos on your own." Then Kratos saw Teknon's wound. "What happened to your arm?"

Teknon placed his hand back on the cut and winced. "We had an unexpected meeting with a well-known pest."

"Scandalon!" Tor exclaimed, his jaw fixed. "Sooner or later, I'm going to get that mindless wind-up toy in my sights. Did Phil jump in?"

"He sure did," Teknon said, nodding at Phil. "You surprised me with that torpedo move, Phil. How do you do that drilling thing anyway?"

"All Phaskos have the ability to travel under the ground faster than we can above it."

"Now I know why you wear those multi-toothed gloves of yours." Teknon ran his hand over one of Phil's armored arms.

Kratos looked closely at Teknon's arm. "As soon as Epps gets back, we'll have him fix that."

Teknon shook his head. "No thanks, Dad." "We can bandage it. I think I'll keep this one."

Tor affectionately put his large hand on Teknon's shoulder. "To remind you of tonight?" he asked, smiling. Teknon nodded with a grin. "Good!" Tor added, with a proud tone in his voice. "Look at the mark often, and remember what you've learned through this experience. Never forget that tonight you looked your fear in the face and conquered it!"

"And you recovered," Kratos said. "I know you felt that you had failed in our encounter with the footsoldiers, but you recovered from those feelings of failure." Then he turned back to Phil. "Speaking of facing fear, do you still have the quad-level chessmatrix set we used to play?"

"Indeed I do," Phil said, looking at Kratos slyly. "But I think you should come back and enjoy a good meal before challenging me again."

Suddenly a voice came over Kratos' communication device. "Captain, Matty here."

"Go ahead, Mat."

"We've got the kids, and they're fine."

Kratos saw relief pass across Phil's face, then he responded, "That's great!"

Matty continued, "You'd better get back here before the food is gone. I'd hate to see what would happen if Tor didn't get anything to eat."

"On our way, Speedster," Kratos replied.

The four of them headed for the village.

GOOD ENOUGH?

A hearty meal with the Phaskos and a good night's sleep revived the team for the next leg of its journey to Magos' headquarters. The team spent the next few days hiking on a trail toward the Northron Peninsula, which lay north of Hedon Bay and at the foot of the Thumos Mountains. Magos had set up his fortress in the heart of the mountains—a strategic location in the event of a battle. Kratos wanted to reach the village of Northros as quickly as possible in order to establish a temporary base before attempting to enter the treacherous mountain region.

Phil was now a permanent member of the team. He disclosed his association with Kratos to the other Phaskos on the night of the Lacerlazer incident. Phil knew that, unlike himself, the Phaskos guarded their reclusive lifestyle and did not like their privacy disrupted. Now that Phil had identified his relationship with Kratos, the rest of the small mining clan would become wary that Magos and his henchman might soon return for the informant. Phil's kinsmen, as expected, were relieved to see him depart with the rest of the team the following morning.

En route to Northros, Teknon pumped his father with questions about his relationship with Phil. To Teknon's surprise, Kratos and Phil had known each other since engineering school more than 20 years earlier. Although born on Kairos, Phil was sent to Basileia as a child by his poverty-stricken mother who could not support him. Fortunately he was adopted from an orphanage by two wealthy and dedicated Basileian parents. Phil went on to excel at the finest schools, including BTI—the Basileia Technology Institute. There he was assigned to room with another young, brilliant, engineering student named Kratos.

The two became friends immediately. During the next few years at the institute, they spent many late nights sipping nela while discussing everything from engineering to theology. Both were students and followers of the CHAMPION Warrior doctrine. Upon graduation, they reluctantly parted company. Kratos remained on Basileia while Phil returned to make a difference for his people on Kairos. Through the years, however, they had continued to visit each other, sharing ideas and brainstorming on several new technologies of their own design. Together, they teamed up to create the ultimate weapon for what they hoped would be a new legion of CHAMPION Warriors.

"You mean Phil helped you build the Hoplon?" Teknon asked.

"Not only did he aid in the design," Kratos replied, "he also provided the carbonite alloy for its structure from his mines. It's the hardest material in the system."

Phil smiled. "Only the best for a man who, on occasion, actually beats me at chessmatrix."

"I'll look forward to picking up that gauntlet later," Kratos replied.

The team arrived on the outskirts of Northros early that afternoon. From a distance, they could see the coastline of the beautiful community—white sand dotted with tropical trees swaying in the soothing breeze from the bay. After pausing a moment to appreciate the scenery, they turned their attention to something different.

"I'm starved," Tor said. "Where can we get a meal?"

"You won't have to go far," Phil replied. "The food around Northros is plentiful and grows throughout the city. Just pick what you want."

"Pick what?" Epps asked.

"Anything," Phil said.

"Where?" Arti inquired.

"Anywhere," Phil responded.

"What do you mean? Aren't there any places to go and eat?" Matty questioned.

"None," Phil answered.

"No restaurants? No cafés?" Epps added.

"The community is totally self-sustaining," Phil continued. "Food grows on its own without tending. And that's just the beginning. There are both hot and cold running springs, which provide water to the community. Lodging is available to anyone in perfectly constructed, natural cave dwellings. Basically, when you live in Northros, everything required to live is already provided."

"So," Arti added, "can I assume that living in an ecologically perfect environment, with no concerns for food or shelter, gives the Northrons freedom to pursue other worthwhile goals and endeavors?"

"Freedom, yes, pursue, no," Phil replied, sadly shaking his head.

Tor frowned. "Then what kind of work do they do?"

"*Work?*" Phil responded. "Did I say *work?* Who heard me say *work?*"

"Land it, Phil," Matty said. "What exactly are you trying to say?"

"I'm saying that these are a people whose purpose is summed up in a phrase they use more often than any other. That phrase is 'Good enough.' Northrons don't work; neither do they seek to better themselves. They waste all of their time and intelligence on the pursuit of leisure. In other words, they enjoy mediocrity. The food that grows everywhere is not only perfectly nutritious, it also produces perfectly healthy bodies. Every Northron has a faultless physique and beautiful features.

They have everything they need. Well, almost everything."

"What could they possibly be missing?" Teknon asked in disbelief.

"I'll tell you what they're missing," Tor interjected in his deepest voice. "They have no vision. No purpose. No plan. Where there's no purpose, there's no passion for living. I'm sickened by the thought of it."

Kratos, listening to the discussion and observing Teknon's reaction to it, interrupted. "Well, at least Northros will be a good place to set up a temporary base before we venture into the mountains. Let's find some dinner, get a place to stay, and plan our strategy for tomorrow. Agreed?" Everyone nodded.

Later at their dwelling, dinner was simple but delicious. Fruits and vegetables of all colors, shapes, and sizes hung on trees within arm's reach. Even cooking was unnecessary. After picking a large, yellow, egg-shaped fruit, Teknon bit into it. "This is incredible," he said enthusiastically. "It's like nothing I've ever tasted."

"According to my research," Phil said, chuckling as he munched on a blue, spongy vegetable, "none of this food has any elements that will contribute to excessive weight gain, disease, or hair loss." Then he smiled and patted his smooth head. "Great news for me, don't you think?"

"Sounds like my kind of cafeteria," Matty said. "Speaking of hair, I wonder if I'll get a higher gloss after I eat this stuff."

Kratos began the planning session. "Here's the agenda for tomorrow. In the morning, Matty and I will do some scouting of the mountain region. Once we determine exactly where Magos is set up and which defenses he has in place, we can plan a strategy to penetrate his fortress."

Teknon was surprised to hear that his father was leaving without him. "How long will you be gone?" he inquired.

"Five days," Kratos replied. "We need enough time to get a complete overview of the area."

Teknon continued to probe. "I understand why Matty's going. He can cover the ground in no time. But what are you going to do while he's zipping from one end of the mountains to the other?"

"I'm taking an alternate route," Kratos said with smile, still looking down.

"Which route?" Teknon asked, his frustration building.

"You'll see in the morning," his father responded.

Teknon put his hands on his hips and looked over at Phil. "It bugs me when Dad gets dramatic," Teknon said. "Ever known him to be any different?" Phil asked with a wink.

"Just wait, Tek," Matty added. "Believe me, you're going to love this!"

"Time to hit the sack, gentlemen," Tor said, leaning over and blowing out the lamp. "I can't believe these people are too lazy to build an illumination station so that we can get some decent light around here." He lay down and closed his eyes. "Good night, all," he said, yawning.

*   *   *

As the sun rose on a typically beautiful Northros morning, the team was on a remote section of beach. Kratos and Matty prepared for their departure while the rest of the team gathered around for a few last words. Teknon had not slept well the night before as he had anticipated his father traveling the next five days in enemy territory. He hung back during the conversation on the beach, watching his father confidently give the others instructions to carry out while he and Matty were gone. Teknon also watched his father finish his time with the team by leading them in a heartfelt request to Pneuma for wisdom and strength.

Teknon had always loved and respected his father, but this mission had given him an entirely new perspective on his dad's vision and purpose in life. The youth saw time and time again that Kratos lived by the values he preached. But although Kratos had often shared his convictions with Teknon through the years, the boy still had not completely embraced his father's vision for life. Teknon admired his father's beliefs but he never understood how they applied to his life in a practical way. During this journey, however, Teknon was beginning to see just how important those convictions were to his father and what those convictions meant to the future of Basileia.

Teknon watched as Matty adjusted his shoes in preparation for takeoff. The youth shook his head and chuckled to himself as his swift mentor looked at his own reflection in the water to make sure his collar was straight and his hair in place. All attention then shifted to Kratos as the emblem on his harness glowed and he removed the Hoplon from his back.

"What's happening now?" Teknon asked.

"You'll see," Phil said, looking at Teknon out of the corner of his eye.

Kratos took the shield in his hands and placed it face up on the ground. He then stepped on the Hoplon, placing one foot on either side of the circular object. The elegant CW in the center of the shield faced toward the morning sky. Immediately foot guards that before were invisible enclosed the fronts of both feet. Each side of the Hoplon seemed to separate from the center and sleek, tapered wings began to emerge.

"What in the world?" Teknon exclaimed, his eyes wide.

Before he could complete his sentence, the Hoplon raised two meters above the ground. Kratos stood on top of the shield, smiling broadly at his son.

"Don't tell me," Teknon said, "you can fly on this thing?!"

"All I have to do is think where I want to go," Kratos replied. "The Hoplon does the rest! What do you think?"

"How does it leave the ground?" Teknon asked.

Phil answered Teknon. "The shield creates a cushion between it and the ground. It propels itself with the same energy it created when the force field is engaged. It's like a giant hand carrying it through the air."

"No wonder you didn't tell me about this earlier. I'd have pestered you every minute for a ride."

"You'll get your chance soon enough, Son," Kratos replied. "But for now, Matty has to hit the trail, and I've got to get to the skies."

Teknon looked up at his father, trying to hold back his emotions. "Take care, Dad."

"I love you, Son," Kratos said fondly. He looked at the mentors and Phil. "Watch out for him, guys. And watch out for yourselves. You never know when someone or something is going to pop up."

"We'll be on guard, you can count on that," Tor stated confidently.

"Safe travels, my friends," Epps added.

"Remember, Arti," Kratos said, "we'll contact you through the Sensatron once a day. If we communicate any more than that, Magos will find a way to intercept the transmissions and be alerted to our plans. Use the Alpha code. The Hoplon is invisible on scanners, but who knows what new defense technologies Magos has developed."

"I'll try to get as much information as I can from the locals," Phil said, "but I'm not hopeful, considering their indifference to *any* issues."

"All right, then, " Kratos said, "we're off!" He waved to the others, rose into the sky, and disappeared over the horizon before anyone could return the gesture.

"Later, gents," Matty said grinning. "Save me some of those purple things we ate last night. They put quite a shine on my smile." Tor slapped his friend affectionately on the back. Then Matty vanished in a blur.

That afternoon, the remaining team members sat on the porch of their chambers, overlooking the bay. Teknon watched as several Northrons roamed the majestic shoreline, only a stone's throw away from where he stood. Teknon and his companions had spent the earlier part of the day in the village. Now they were discussing their responsibilities and waiting for the first transmission from Kratos and Matty.

Phil, sampling more local cuisine, noticed Tor brooding by himself in a corner and probed his enormous friend. "What's eating you, Tor?" he asked between bites. "Getting cabin fever already?"

"The Northrons ... " Tor grumbled, "they drive me crazy. Today, down in the village, I asked one of them for directions to the hot-water mineral springs. He pointed and said it was somewhere down the path. When I asked if he could be more specific, he said not to worry, his advice was 'good enough.'" Tor walked to the edge of the porch. "A little later, I walked by a lady carrying a basket of fruit. She accidentally dropped it, spilling the contents. I stopped to help her. Another Northron passed by, but he didn't stop. When I asked him to pick up one piece of fruit that was out of my reach, he told me that I was helping the lady and that was 'good enough.' I tell you, Phil, this I-don't-give-a-rip attitude isn't part of my makeup. I can't handle it."

"Don't say I didn't warn you," Phil said. "Frustrating, isn't it? Somehow I knew the Northrons' passiveness and indecisiveness would bother you more than the others."

Teknon, listening to the conversation, reclined on his chair. He enjoyed looking at the clear water as the waves crashed on the sand in perfect rhythm. He wondered how his father was doing as he flew around the frigid terrain in the mountains. *I wish he would check in*, Teknon thought.

"Arti, any contact?" Teknon asked.

"Not yet," Arti replied. "It's still a bit early."

Teknon crossed his arms and watched several Northrons swimming playfully in the waves. All of the men were tall and muscular and the women's bodies were trim and feminine. *Phil was right; they are a good-looking bunch of people*, Teknon thought.

Epps was also watching the activity on the beach. "They seem to take their health completely for granted," he commented. "Most people have to watch what they eat and exercise constantly to look like that. For them, it's an unearned benefit."

Teknon shaded his eyes as he looked out over the water. He thought he saw something just beyond the breaking waves. It looked like a large shadow underneath the water's surface. *Probably just a reflection from a cloud*, he thought. Then the form appeared again, this time with a definite shape. It was moving toward shore. Teknon slowly stood up and walked toward Tor. Suddenly, the huge form broke the surface. It was large—very large—and it was moving toward the Northron swimmers. Teknon could say nothing, but put his hand on Tor's arm and pointed toward the water.

Tor's eyes widened. "What in the name of ... ?" he yelled. The others heard Tor's words and turned around to look.

Phil, squinting into the sun, dropped his fruit on the floor. "It's a leviathan!" he yelled.

"A what?" Epps asked.

At that moment, the creature extended itself out of the water, revealing its immense size and frightful appearance. It had a reptilian head and razor-like, symmetrical teeth. The beast raised two large claws high into the air and it wailed a deafening screech. Although its lower body remained underwater, the tip of a serpentine tail splashed back and forth.

"Leviathans are the most feared predators in these waters," Phil said, responding to Epps. "This one looks like an adult. It must be 50 meters long."

"Look!" Teknon shouted. "It's heading toward the swimmers!"

The leviathan, closing in on a potential meal, glided closer to one of the women and opened its massive claw. She screamed while the other Northrons abandoned her and swam frantically toward shore.

"Let's move!" Tor called out as he leaped off the porch and onto the beach. The others immediately followed.

Phil grabbed his gloves and shifted his body into the digging mode. Moments later, he was racing underground toward the creature. Tor, Arti, and Epps halted in unison on the shoreline. Tor raised his fists into the air and shot a beam of energy toward the leviathan. The beam wrapped around the beast's claw just before it grasped the young lady. Tor focused his concentration and pulled back on the beam with all his might. The creature swayed off balance but still managed to swing its massive tail and wrap it around the girl. Epps dove into the water and swam as fast as he could, hoping to reach the creature in time to touch it with his gloves.

Tor pulled again, this time in an alternate direction. The leviathan finally released its grip on the girl and she tumbled into the surf. Teknon, seeing his chance, reacted instantly.

The creature now turned its attention to Tor. With a quick motion, the leviathan spun around, swung Tor into the air using his own energy beams, and grasped the warrior with its unhindered claw. Tor grimaced as the massive claw sur-

rounded him and began to squeeze. Arti saw his friend's dilemma and, within seconds, shot a beam from his face band. The beam hit the leviathan directly in the face, and the creature stopped moving. Arti kept firing as Epps dove under the water and closed in on the creature.

After struggling through the turbulent surf, Teknon reached the young Northron and pulled her to shore. He checked her breathing and her pulse, and examined her quickly to make sure she wasn't bleeding. She was unconscious, but stable. He carried her to a grove of trees, then ran back to help his friends.

Epps fought underwater currents caused by the flailing of the leviathan's tail. He repeatedly reached for the creature, only to be thrown back by the force of the churning water. He knew he had to touch the leviathan soon or Tor would be finished. Holding his breath, Epps dove to the bottom and positioned himself with legs bent, waiting for the right moment. The leviathan's tail swung low in the water, and Epps pushed up hard. His fingers almost touched the creature, but not quite. Suddenly a form emerged from within a swirl of sand on the bottom and quickly grabbed Epps by the legs.

Phil's body propelled through the water like a missile. He pushed Epps' body until he was able to reach the leviathan. Epps extended his arms as far as he could and finally grabbed the creature's tail firmly with both hands. His gloves glowed brightly in the dark-blue water. The creature turned violently and pulled Epps through the water, but Epps kept his grip.

Meanwhile, Arti kept his beam fixed on the leviathan's forehead. The combination of Arti's ray and Epps' gloves began to affect the huge creature. The claw released its grip on Tor, and the warrior fell feet first into the water. Phil burrowed back to shore and popped up next to Teknon. Both Arti and Epps could sense that the creature was weakening. Swaying back and forth, the leviathan finally gave up its efforts and fell back hard into the water. Epps released his grip and shot toward the surface to refill his lungs. Arti turned off his beam and began looking for Tor and Epps. Tor, a bit shaken, had dragged himself up onto dry land as soon as the beast released him.

When the team reunited on the beach, each congratulated the other for the victory and their effort. After a few minutes, however, Tor's face darkened and his temper began to surface. "Where were the emergency teams? What happened to the Northrons who ran away?"

"I told you," Phil responded. "They have no emergency teams because no one wants to make the effort. They just don't care."

Teknon went to the tree under which the young Northron was recuperating. She was sitting up when Teknon arrived. "You okay?" Teknon asked.

"I'm fine," she responded. "I guess I owe a lot to you guys!"

"Don't thank me," Teknon said as he checked her pulse and looked in the direction of his friends. "Thank those guys over there who risked their necks for you." The girl nodded. Teknon carefully helped her to her feet, and they walked slowly over to the rest of the team.

Epps saw her coming and went to her side. "Well, little lady, not a typical day at the beach for you, I suspect," he said as he placed his gloves on her shoulders to search for injuries.

"Not exactly," she responded. Epps smiled and nodded to Teknon that she was unhurt. Teknon returned a grin.

Phil looked over the girl's shoulder and watched the Northrons who had deserted her. They were casually walking toward the group, but none of them seemed distressed about the incident or concerned about their friend.

"Why don't we all go back to the cave and refresh ourselves?" Phil suggested. "I think I've found a way to squeeze the juice out of some of these delectable fruits. Come, my friends." Phil took Tor's arm and started pulling him away just as the Northrons walked up.

"Hey, how ya doin', Pary?" one of the young men asked.

"Fine," the girl answered. She pointed to the team. "These guys pulled me away from that *thing*."

"Good enough," another young man said, nodding. He walked over to Pary to lead her back to the beach.

Tor turned abruptly. Still drenched in seawater, he trudged over to one of the tall, attractive Northrons. The warrior put his face directly in front of the young man's face. "Good enough, did you say?" Tor snarled through gritted teeth. "We almost got killed out there trying to save this girl, and all you've got to say is, 'good enough'?"

"Sure!" the Northron responded. "You saved her, she's fine, and everything's at peace. What else? It's good enough."

Arti tried to cut in. "Tor, this is not a productive conversation. Let's go."

Arti's words didn't register with Tor. He was too focused on the individual in front of him. "What else?" Tor said, his nose almost touching the Northron's nose. "I'll tell you what else, you spineless, indecisive, passionless slug. Where were you when your friend was facing death? Where are your beach patrols? Where are your hospitals, your schools, your places of worship?" Tor startled the Northron by grabbing his shirt. "What else? Here's what else!" In one effortless motion, Tor picked up the Northron and threw him to one side. The Northron flew through the air, his arms and legs flailing. He landed hard on the sand, then sat motionless holding his head in his hands.

Tor, looking back at the young man on the sand, drew in a deep breath and regained his composure. Epps, shaking his head in disbelief, walked calmly to the Northron and examined him.

Arti, watching Epps treat his patient, exhorted Tor. "Now do you believe that we should have left? Do you feel better now?"

Tor's anger slowly softened to embarrassment. "There I go again," he said humbly.

Teknon watched as Pary also walked over to the injured Northron. Epps completed the treatment by applying his gloves.

"Good thing this fellow has such excellent muscle structure," Epps said, placing his gloves on the Northron. "The damage could have been much worse."

Arti spoke sternly to Tor. "What do you think the Logos would reveal about your temper?"

"I blew it, clear and simple. It never pays to let my emotions get away from me. I know I've got a temper. But as a

CHAMPION Warrior, I've got to learn to manage my anger."
Tor looked sheepishly at Epps as the physician returned to
the group. "How's he doing?" Tor asked.

"He had a mild concussion," Epps responded. "No problem
mending that one. But I think there's one more wound to
heal, don't you, Tor?"

Tor again sighed deeply and started walking toward the
Northron. "Where's he going?" Teknon asked. "He's not going
to start things up with the Northron again, is he?"

"He's going to apologize," Phil said. "Tor knows that one
of the marks of a CHAMPION is the willingness to ask forgiveness when you've offended another person." Teknon
carefully watched as Tor reached the Northron, who was
fully recuperated.

"What's up, big guy?" The Northron said, standing up
and smiling. "Wanna throw me to the other side of the
beach this time?"

"I had no right to treat you as I did," Tor said kindly. "I've
come to apologize. Will you forgive me for hurting you?"

Teknon walked over to Epps and commented, "It's strange
watching a warrior like Tor humble himself like that."

"We all have areas of struggle when it comes to self-control,"
Epps responded. "Tor's temper is his trouble spot. He's getting
a handle on it, but every day is a challenge. Today he lost it, but
at least he's doing the right thing by asking forgiveness. That's
a sign of true strength."

"How did it go?" Phil asked as Tor returned from his conversation with the Northron.

"Well, he accepted my apology. In his own way, of course."

"No. You don't mean—did he say ... ?"

"Yeah," Tor interrupted Arti, shaking his head with a blank
expression. "He told me, 'Good enough.'"

THE ELEMENT OF DOUBT

Magos walked slowly down the wide halls of his headquarters, a colossal fortress he called Sheol. This
castle of war stood in the most treacherous region of the
Thumos Mountains. Legions of footsoldiers guarded the
perimeter of Sheol, which itself was surrounded by an invisible energy field. The energy field protected Sheol's inhabi-
tants from the fierce snow and wind that continually ripped
through the surrounding area.

The fortress displayed a dark, smooth, almost crystalline
appearance, and was composed of three towering structures.
Magos spent most of his time in the top of the middle tower,
the nucleus of his technological empire. But few people ever
had the chance, or the desire, to see Sheol—even at a distance.

Kairos was a land of atmospheric extremes. Although
Northros enjoyed a consistently perfect climate, the weather in
the Thumos Mountain range, north and west of Northros, was
completely different. No one in the low country dared to trav-

el across the mountains. Sub-zero temperatures, ice storms, and roaming packs of large, carnivorous creatures kept any outsiders from exploring the Thumos territory, which allowed Magos to enjoy complete isolation from his enemies.

Whenever he passed, footsoldiers and kakos alike stopped what they were doing and lowered their heads in submission. Magos had designed his creatures to treat him like the master he desired to be, a ruler with complete control and dominion. As he walked through Sheol on this occasion, his elaborately ornate garments gave him the mystical appearance of a sorcerer. As he stopped in front of an enormous, impenetrable door, the fixture on the side of his head began to glow, triggering the two panels of the door to slide open.

Magos walked inside. The cavernous room was almost completely empty except for a solitary light that shone around a small, spherical object in the room's center. He continued to approach until he penetrated the lighted field, then paused to look at the small sphere sitting on its multi-pronged perch. The sphere was intricately complex in design and beautiful in appearance. Magos paced slowly around the object, his brow tightening with anger. Soon he stopped and gazed directly through the light. Within the sphere, Magos saw beautiful and radiant images swirling in a cloud of colors. It was the Logos.

The Logos held all of the teachings and records of the original CHAMPION Warriors. After the Warriors disbanded decades earlier, the Logos was created as the only complete archive of the CHAMPION beliefs. To access the teachings, a person had to place his hand on the Logos. This action produced an image of a CHAMPION instructor.

Magos stood motionless for several minutes, as he gazed into the heart of the Logos. He had many opportunities to learn from the Logos early in his life. His parents had offered to take him to see it on many occasions. But Magos chose otherwise. Instead, he allowed other, more practical interests to prevent him from taking time to learn the CHAMPION principles for living.

Although Magos had gained superior strength and intelligence through his transformation, he had sacrificed the ability to connect on a spiritual level with the Warrior King, known to the CHAMPION Warriors as Pneuma. Magos was partially human, but that was a temporary situation. Ultimately, he desired to replace the remainder of his human structure with electronic circuitry. He knew that such a reality would allow him to live forever without pain or illness, but also knew that his extended life would lack the joy and peace experienced within a divinely created spirit. Magos had not anticipated this devastating side-effect when he chose to become a machine. This unexpected limitation created continuous anger in him, and he was consumed with controlling those who were not so limited.

With knowledge comes power, Magos thought. *If I can learn the deepest secrets of the CHAMPION convictions, I can twist and distort them. Then I can confuse the people of Basileia with a different philosophy, one that better suits my purpose.*

As Magos continued to brood, another figure quietly entered the room. Magos remained motionless as the individual silently drew closer to him. Magos detected the intruder's entrance, but said nothing. Finally, another face broke through the lighted field. It was *Kratos'* face! The figure stood motionless behind Magos, its eyes empty and fixed forward. For several moments, both of them remained silent.

Magos finally broke the silence. "Well, what have you to report?"

"Master, two of the warriors are scouting in the mountains," the android responded. "The others remain in Northros."

Magos turned around. He was face to face with Dolios, the android Magos designed to guard the Logos. Magos produced a slight grin as he looked carefully at his creation. "When I see you standing there, Dolios, I have an intense urge to vaporize you on the spot."

"Of course," Dolios responded, expressionless. "That's why you choose for me to appear in this form. To remind you of your hatred for Kratos."

"Partially," Magos replied, slowly turning toward the Logos. "But there are other reasons your appearance invigorates me. Although I hate everything he stands for, I still want Kratos at my side. Seeing his likeness in you reminds me how much I want to conquer Kratos and transform him into my likeness."

Magos folded his robotic arms. "I've tested his abilities. I know his purpose. I also know now how powerful he is when he combines his efforts with his team. I must allow Kratos and his companions to reach Sheol. This is my stronghold, my position of strength." As Magos spoke, the reflection of the Logos appeared in the lens of the transocular implant that had replaced his right eye. "When they come here," he said with a venomous snarl, "I'll separate them. Then I will destroy each of those warriors one by one, except Kratos. He will fulfill his destiny by helping me to conquer the galaxy, beginning with his beloved Basileia." Magos clenched his huge fist, holding it up to the Logos. "And nothing, but nothing, will stop me from having him." Dolios continued to stand at attention behind his master.

"Which warriors are scouting?" Magos asked, his speech quickening.

"The one called Mataios is covering the ground, while Kratos continues to perform aerial surveillance."

"I believe it's time to make an impression on my old partner," Magos replied. "An indirect approach may be most appropriate." He hesitated. "Kratos needs a deeper understanding of my purpose. No doubt, the best way to influence the father will be through his son." When Magos finished his statement, the antenna on his head was glowing. A small probe flew into the room, barely missing Dolios as it zoomed past. The saucer-shaped object hummed quietly as it hovered close to Magos' face. A pale-green light gleamed from the probe and illuminated Magos' distorted features as he conveyed his evil intent to his obedient creation.

"Find Kratos' son," Magos said firmly. "Alert me when he's located. I have a message to deliver." Small lights flashed on the flying messenger as it flew quickly out of the room and exited Sheol through a portal on the exterior wall that opened for it. Magos watched his probe as it sped toward its destination. Then he turned around and walked slowly out of the room, leaving Dolios still at attention.

*   *   *

Back in Northros, Teknon escorted the young Northron lady home after her alarming experience with the leviathan. Tor had instructed Teknon to come back to the cave after assisting her. Teknon enjoyed talking with his new acquaintance as they walked. Their conversation reminded him that he missed his friends on Basileia. He was weary of the recent training and intense activity, and felt like he needed a break from adults. It was great to meet someone his own age.

"By the way," Teknon said, sheepishly, "you didn't tell me your name. Did I hear your friend at the beach call you Pary?"

"Paranomia," the girl responded, "but most people call me Pary."

"Pary," Teknon repeated. "That's a name I've never heard before. But I like it."

"Thanks," Pary said. "I've never met anyone named Teknon either." She looked at him. "So, Teknon," she continued with a warm expression, "what makes you so brave? I've never seen anyone do what your friends did today. I was impressed."

"Oh, it was *good enough*," Teknon said sarcastically, but with a smile. "At least that's what your friend said, right?"

"He's not really my friend," Pary said as her smile disappeared. "He just goes with me to the beach sometimes. I don't have many friends around here, and I can't depend on anybody."

"You don't mean all Northrons are undependable, do you?" Teknon inquired.

Pary frowned and looked away. "Northrons are taught from childhood to think only of themselves, never obliged to keep a commitment. I grew up here, so I guess I'm like that, too. Best to learn now, Teknon, that Northrons never do what they say they'll do."

"Well, how about us?" Teknon responded with pride. "You can depend on us, can't you?"

Pary slowed down and turned toward Teknon. "I don't know. Maybe." She looked into his face, smiling again. "I guess you look pretty dependable." They continued walking to her home.

Later at the cave, Teknon said good night to his friends, closed his bedroom door, and lay down. While the other team members continued to debrief from the day's activities, Teknon thought about the day and especially about his walk with Pary. *She's pretty*, he thought, *and funny too.* Teknon put his hands behind his head and looked out the window. *I'd like to see her again.* Soon the activity and excitement of the day began to catch up with him, and before long, he drifted off to sleep.

After several minutes, Teknon was pulled out of his light sleep by a low, buzzing sound. He opened his eyes slightly and saw a small object fly through his window. Lights danced over the top of the circular probe. Before he could jump out of bed and alert his friends, the object abruptly stopped and hovered directly over his head. Teknon lay still, waiting for the invader's next move.

Suddenly the probe projected a holographic image to the left of Teknon's bed. The image stood large and ominous, appearing to look directly into Teknon's eyes. It spoke to him. "So," Magos said, projecting his image from Sheol, "you're the son of Kratos. I must say, my old partner did a fine job raising his offspring. Oh, by the way, my name is Magos."

Teknon, shaken, tried to keep a calm tone. "Well, I didn't think you were from room service." He pointed to the probe. "What's this thing doing here? What do you want?"

"Simply to offer you a proposition, young warrior," Magos said, his image appearing to walk around the foot of the bed.

"A proposition?" Teknon said, anxiously trying to sit up. "What could I possibly want from you?"

"Well, Teknon," Magos said, stepping closer, "I think you are proceeding from the assumption that I intend to harm you and your companions. Is that true?"

"What else?" Teknon responded, with anger rising in his voice. "After we almost got blown away by a monster storm? After your oversized goons ambushed us? After my father and friends almost got zapped in an energy field? I wouldn't exactly call those great references!" Teknon started to get out

of bed. "Shouldn't I get the others?" he said nervously. "I'm sure they'd like to be included in this conversation. They've probably heard us already."

Magos smiled. "Not likely. This probe is creating a sound barrier around the room. You can talk as loud as you like." Magos' changed his expression and tone to one of counterfeit concern. "I apologize for your difficulties. The mishaps you experienced on the way were simply the responses of an auto-mated defense system. When I realized it was Kratos and his team who were involved, I turned off the system immediately. Teknon, do you realize what a huge mistake your father is making by refusing to join me? He and I were once partners, you know."

Teknon interrupted, "I know all about it. You went berserk and decided to become some sort of digitized dictator. Dad told me how you want to conquer Basileia and become its ruler."

"A slanted perspective," Magos said. "I came up here to continue the research your father and I started on Basileia. I needed a new facility with seclusion to perfect the technology we created years ago. It was technology designed to help oth-ers." Magos' image turned slightly and pointed a long finger toward the window. "But up in those mountains, I've suc-ceeded in completing the biosynthetic matrix." The cyborg paused for a moment, then opened both hands to Teknon. "Teknon, how would you like to have a flawless body? A new body—one that would last forever. Think of it. You would never grow old. You would never die!"

"Not on your artificial life," stated Teknon. "Why would I want to look like you?"

"But that's the point. You wouldn't look like me. I've per-fected the process. You could look like anything you wanted. You could look so good that Pary or any other woman couldn't resist you."

Surprised, Teknon started thinking. *How could he know about Pary? What does he mean I could have a flawless body, one that wouldn't wear out? A body that I could design? No, no, that can't be true.*

Teknon refocused his full attention on Magos. "I'm not interested in your new matrix. My father and I follow the teachings of the CHAMPION Warriors. The Warriors teach exactly the opposite of what you're talking about. That's why we're going to get the Logos and take it back to Basileia where it belongs."

"Yes, of course, the Logos," Magos said calmly. "An important relic to be sure. But are you certain about the reliability of the CHAMPION teachings? Are you positive that my objectives are different from yours? Aren't we all committed to the happiness of mankind? Don't we all want to live longer, more productive lives? Do you realize that years ago the CHAMPION philosophy was considered restrictive and extreme? That's why Basileians decided they didn't need it anymore. After decades of CHAMPION oppression, the people came up with their own philosophy, one that made them happier. That's when your father and I developed our technology to help people enjoy longer, happier lives. But he left before it was completed."

Teknon's mind started racing. *What am I thinking? Why is he starting to make sense? Why am I unsure whether or not the CHAMPION teachings are different from his? Why don't I know what to say to him?*

Teknon spoke, this time sounding a little less sure of himself. "This conversation is over. Either you call this metallic firefly back to your base, or I'll have one of my friends come in and turn it into a frying pan."

Magos grinned. "That's won't be necessary. Consider what we've discussed. We're not so different, your father and I. The possibilities for you, Teknon, are endless. Think on that, young warrior."

As soon as Magos finished talking, the lights on the probe changed their pattern. The holographic image faded, and the probe flew out of the window before Teknon could utter another word. He lay back in bed with his eyes open wide. Questions raced through his mind almost as fast as his heart was beating. He lay motionless for several seconds before jumping out of bed and running into the other room. In a few minutes he had explained the surprise visit from Magos to his companions.

The following morning Teknon left soon after breakfast to visit Pary. Tor granted Teknon's request to visit the young lady, but instructed him to make contact every hour. Teknon walked briskly on the path to Pary's house. On the way his mind was filled with the issues Magos brought up during their conversation. Teknon was frustrated that he didn't have an adequate response for Magos. The mentors had tried to explain the flaws in Magos' plan, but Teknon remained unsure. He wished he could talk with his father to clear up the confusion. Kratos, however, was not scheduled to return for another three days.

Suddenly Teknon stopped his train of thought. He was tired of being frustrated and wanted to have some fun for a change; so, he decided to think about a much more pleasant topic, namely his upcoming visit.

During the next few days, Teknon spent a lot of time with Pary. The two hiked over much of the Northron Peninsula. Each morning Teknon rose early, ate breakfast, and ran out the door to meet his new friend. He either met Pary at her house or at a predetermined location, like the beach. Pary showed Teknon all of her favorite places around the area, including mountain trails and hidden lakes that few people visited.

Pary and Teknon didn't ask anyone else to come along with them because they enjoyed being alone with each other. From dawn to dusk the two talked, laughed, and shared everything about each other's lives. They talked about their likes and dislikes, their dreams, and their hopes for the future. Teknon didn't even pull back when Pary started holding his hand, even though it felt strange.

After the second day, the mentors began to wonder if Teknon was spending too much time with the young Northron. They didn't want to infringe on his enjoyment by forbidding the two from seeing each other, but they also wanted Teknon to keep his focus on the mission at hand. On the third day, the day Kratos and Matty planned to return, Epps made sure he was up before Teknon left.

"Up early again, Teknon?" Epps said wiping the sleep from his eyes. Teknon nodded as he quickly gobbled a piece of fruit by candlelight. It was still dark outside.

"Where are you and Pary heading today?" Epps inquired, sitting down by Teknon.

"We'll be all over the place," Teknon said, gobbling a mouthful of food. "First we're going body-surfing at the far end of the beach. Then we're off to see an incredible view of the bay from a cliff Pary knows about. If we have time, we'll finish the day with a swim in a lake she calls The Hidden Gem." Teknon leaned back and smiled as he wiped his mouth. "Quite a day ahead, huh Epps?"

"I'll say," Epps replied, also leaning back.

"Well, I'm gone," Teknon said as he stood up. He grabbed his shirt and turned toward the door. "See ya later."

Before Teknon took another step, he felt the hand of his mentor firmly on his arm. "Not so fast, Teknon." Epps said.

"But I told Pary I'd meet her in 15 minutes," Teknon said anxiously.

"I know. But we need to talk about your relationship with Pary."

Teknon looked surprised. "Relationship? What relationship? You make it sound like Pary and I have some kind of boyfriend-girlfriend thing going on."

"Well?" Epps inquired, "don't you?"

"Epps," Teknon said, still wanting to get out the door, "you've got to be kidding. We're just having a little fun. I'm finally getting a breather from all of this extreme CHAMPION stuff. What's the harm in that?"

Epps looked intently at Teknon. "There's no harm in having a little fun. But do you think Pary feels the same way? I saw you walking hand in hand with her on the beach yesterday. Do you think anyone around here would show her such attention and genuine affection? Don't you think her emotions are starting to get involved?

"And what about you? Aren't you getting a little too distracted from our purpose here? We've had to brief you quickly the past two nights on your father's transmissions before you dropped in bed from exhaustion. Kratos is due back in a few hours. Don't you want to stay and greet him and to hear what he's discovered in the mountains?"

Teknon stopped tugging from Epps' grip and sat down. He rubbed his face for a few seconds, like it was helping him to think. Then he looked at Epps. "I have been distracted, haven't I?" he said quietly. "I almost forgot Dad was coming back today. I've been having so much fun with Pary, I just let everything else go. He paused, then looked directly at Epps. "I guess it's time for a reality check."

"I know this mission has been rough on you," Epps said, putting his hand on Teknon's arm again. "But you can't forget why we're here. And you certainly can't lead Pary to believe you care romantically for her just because you want to escape from the real world for a few days."

Teknon blew out a deep sigh. "You're right. Ever since that visit from Magos, I've been trying to forget how confused he made me feel. I couldn't defend my position, Epps! It bothered me that Magos actually started making sense! Maybe he wasn't really making sense, but I didn't know enough about what the CHAMPION Warriors taught to tell him differently. I didn't even know enough about what I believed, for that matter."

"The element of doubt bothers you, doesn't it?" Epps said, smiling.

"The what?" Teknon asked.

"Magos wanted to create doubt in your mind about your beliefs so that you would feel frightened and insecure. He knows that you're young in your convictions, and he wants to take advantage of that. I'm sure Kratos was also a factor in his visit."

"Dad," Teknon questioned, "What did he have to do with it?"

"Magos knows that if he can confuse and tempt you, your father will become concerned. Kratos will be occupied with the influence Magos has on your thoughts and actions. Then your father will be distracted and more open to attack.

Remember, above all, Magos wants to defeat your father."

Teknon eyes narrowed. "Why that dirty ... "

"The point is," Epps interrupted, "you've just confronted a basic CHAMPION principle."

"And that is?" Teknon asked, still angry.

"That a CHAMPION Warrior makes the effort to know and understand exactly what he believes so that he can live out those beliefs in the most difficult situations. Magos challenged your beliefs, and you were confused. Now what do you need to do?"

"Study!" Teknon said with conviction. "Study the CHAMPION principles and start living by them. Next time I'll know what to say. No more doubt. I'm not going to let Magos get the upper hand like that again. And I'm not going to let him get to Dad because of my ignorance."

"Good!" Epps said. "Now you've only got one more thing to do before your father gets back."

"Pary?" Teknon asked, wincing. "You really think I've been leading her on?"

"Better go find out," Epps said. "But I'd be prepared to do some serious apologizing if I were you." The mentor got up from the table and started back to the bedroom. "Now, if you'll excuse me, there's a bed in that room that requires my company for another hour. I'll see you later this morning."

"Right," Teknon said. As he walked out the door, Teknon shook his head and thought out loud, "The stupid things you get yourself into."

Teknon saw Pary running toward him as he arrived at the beach. The sun glimmered over the horizon, breaking through the dawn with an explosion of colors. The light shined on Pary's face, and Teknon could see her smile getting bigger as she got closer to him. Because of Teknon's conversation with Epps, he was more sensitive than before to Pary's gestures. So he was more than a little startled when she threw her arms around his neck.

"Hey, fella, where have you been?" Pary asked, holding tightly to him.

"I'm just five minutes late," Teknon responded, his body

stiffening. He forced a smile as he moved his head from underneath her arms. He tried to look calm as he motioned for her to follow him down the beach.

"I missed you so much last night," Pary said, walking closer to him than usual. "I just couldn't get you off my mind."

Teknon's mind started racing. *Epps was right,* he thought. *She wasn't like this yesterday. She's starting to get emotional about our relationship. I can tell right now, this isn't going to be easy.* Teknon barely heard Pary talking as he continued to think.

"Did you hear what I said?" Pary said, smiling as she talked.

"What?" Teknon said, regaining his focus. "I'm sorry, Pary, what was it?"

"I said that next month, when the rainbow seals are running in the harbor, we should pack a bag and watch them swim as the sun comes up. How does that sound?"

Teknon didn't want to start his next sentence. He shook his head a little and tried to force himself to get the first word out of his mouth. Several attempts ended in failure. Finally, he stopped walking and looked up with an embarrassed expression on his face. "Pary," he blurted out, "I won't be around next month. I won't be around next week. I've got to leave soon, maybe even today. I thought you knew that."

Confused, Pary stopped and looked at Teknon. He could already see the hurt starting to surface in her eyes. "What do you mean, you're leaving today?" she said. "I thought ... I thought we were starting to get close."

"We are close, Pary," Teknon responded quickly, trying to row as fast as he could on a sinking ship. "We've become great friends during the past few days, haven't we?"

"Friends?" Pary responded, her eyes starting to moisten. "I traded my favorite pair of earrings to get this swimsuit, just so I could look my best for you today. I could barely sleep last night because I couldn't wait for this morning. I already mentioned to some of the other Northron girls how much I like you, how much I enjoy being with you. Nobody treats me like you have the past few days. Friends? I see you as much more than a friend, Teknon."

Teknon swallowed hard. His silence was louder than the pounding waves on the shore. He was shocked by what he heard. *I thought I was just having a little fun,* he thought. *Obviously that isn't the message I communicated to Pary.* He felt ashamed and regretful, but he didn't know what to say next.

"Pary, I ... " he said, fumbling for words, "I thought we had a great time. You know, a few laughs among friends. I'm sorry ... "

Pary interrupted. "Don't be," she said, regaining her emotions and talking with the firm, indifferent tone she had used before, when Teknon had first walked her home. "I should have known you'd be just like the rest of them. No difference. No difference at all." Pary looked away and closed her eyes tightly. "And what do I care? I'm a Northron, aren't I?" With that, she turned quickly and started walking home.

"Wait a minute, Pary," Teknon said, trying to continue the conversation.

Pary's eyes remained focused forward. "Forget it," she said, her voice trembling. "Just one of those things. See ya."

Teknon started to run after her, but stopped. He knew there wasn't much he could say. He had been insensitive and selfish. Pary had been hurt unnecessarily, and Teknon felt responsible. He turned, his head down, and walked back to meet the other team members.

*   *   *

The others watched and waited for their overdue companions. Tor, arms crossed, scanned the sky, straining to see a sign of Kratos. Epps and Phil walked around nervously.

Arti, still contemplating the readings on his Sensatron, broke into a smile. "I think we're about to have a visitor."

A blur entered the cave and halted in front of Arti. Wind and debris followed the vacuum created when he invaded the room.

"Hi'ya, guys!" Matty exclaimed, smirking and totally relaxed. "Miss me?"

Matty's companions immediately flocked around him, slapping him on the back and flooding him with questions.

Matty's visor snapped back, revealing the cool clarity of his eyes.

Tor's voice rose above the rest as he bellowed a question. "Where is he, Matty? Is he far behind?"

"Not far, big guy," Matty answered. "In fact, why don't you just turn around and ask him yourself?"

Tor twisted his neck in time to see the Hoplon glide over his head, then slowly lower to the ground. The foot guards immediately released, and Kratos stepped off his metallic magic carpet. The Hoplon retracted into its normal size as Kratos picked it up and put it back into its harness. He dusted off his sleeves and beamed. "If I don't get a cup of cold nela in the next five minutes," he said with faked seriousness, "I might have to resort to one of your codlizzard protein shakes, Phil."

Laughter and greetings went on for several minutes until Phil brought out cups of nela for everyone. During the festivities, Kratos noticed that his son was missing from the reunion. "Where's Teknon?" he asked. "Didn't he know that we were arriving this morning?"

"Yes, he did," Epps replied, "but he had some unfinished business to take care of. I expect him back soon." Just then Epps saw a solitary figure enter the cave. "Here I am," Teknon called out. He ran up to Kratos and embraced him, squeezing as tight as his arms would allow. Kratos squeezed back, then held his son by the shoulders.

"What's the matter, Son?" Kratos asked perceptively, trying to talk over the continuing celebration. "Epps said you had some unfinished business. What happened?"

"Let's talk about it later," Teknon said. He felt relieved to see his father safe and unhurt. The two turned toward the others, each taking a cup of nela from Phil. Then they all raised their drinks and toasted to the successful scouting trip.

After everyone took a long sip, Matty grinned broadly and said, "Well, we've seen the target." He looked around the room like he was about to spend money that was burning a hole in his pocket. "Gents, this place makes Kratos' flying fortress on Basileia look like a weather balloon."

With that, the cups went back onto the table, and the team gathered around the weary scouts. It was time to plan for the coming battle.

NOTHING MORE,
NOTHING LESS,
NOTHING ELSE

Kratos and Matty ate a large lunch, then rested for a few hours. The team packed up late in the afternoon and started their trek into the Thumos Mountains. As they reached the edge of Northros, Teknon stopped and turned around. His throat tightened as he looked one last time at the tranquil beachside community. Regret from the incident with Pary battered him like a storm, and his face reflected his inner struggle.

"Time to leave it behind and recover," Kratos said, noticing his son's hesitation. "What's done is done. It's time to focus on the task at hand."

Teknon nodded slowly, then resumed walking up the trail at his father's side. Soon the weather changed dramatically. They became aware of crossing the meteorological dividing line the minute they left Northros. The temperature immediately started to drop and a chilling wind brought blankets of snow. The warriors responded by taking out their insulated thermal jackets.

"It's amazing how quickly the weather changes around here," Epps said, shivering slightly as he fastened the front of his jacket. Three hours into the hike, Kratos signaled for the team to take a short break.

After a few minutes, Kratos pointed to the mentors. "You four go ahead and make sure the paths are clear of footsoldiers. Our scanners may not be accurate in this weather. Phil and Teknon will help me set up camp in the clearing ahead."

"Why don't I shoot ahead alone?" Matty asked, looking up the hill. "I could blanket the area and be back within the hour."

"Nothing doing, Mat," Kratos responded. "It's important for you to stay together. Magos probably knows our position. He might deploy some of his oversized toys to slow us down. I want you to keep each other company."

"Acknowledged!" Tor said, standing up. "We'll see you after dusk." He turned around and barked to his companions, "Let's hit the trail."

In the clearing, Teknon's eyes narrowed to see through the increasing layer of falling snow. Kratos turned on the infra-illuminator just as the sun began to set behind the mountain. The infra-illuminator gave the warriors low-light vision capabilities while preventing detection from enemy surveillance. Phil secured the last fastener on his thermal suit, then started walking toward the woods.

Teknon saw Phil and yelled across the clearing. "Hey, Phil, where are you heading?"

"To find a good spot," Phil responded.

"For what?" Teknon asked.

"Digging, of course." Phil waved as he pushed through the biting snow. "I'll be back in a few minutes."

"Digging?" Teknon said to himself.

Kratos took the Hoplon out of its harness, placed it on the ground, and set it on scan. Then he walked over to the edge of the lighted field and attempted to contact Arti's Sensatron. Teknon, meanwhile, tried to clear as much snow as possible from the ground where he thought he and his companions would eventually put their sleeping pads. As Teknon passed by his father, he saw something moving out of the corner of his eye. Kratos was watching Phil in the distance, as Teknon stopped to take a closer look at the small screen on the shield. His mouth dropped open and he shouted to his father, "Dad, something's coming!" Teknon pointed. "Look, over there!"

Kratos turned just in time to see a massive form emerging from the brush. It grabbed trees in each of its huge hands as it lumbered along, pulling them out of its way and thrusting them to the ground like blades of grass. Teknon strained to view the creature more clearly through the blinding powder that was stinging his face, but all he could see was the outline of a hulking form standing at least 10 meters tall.

Phil surfaced at the other end of the clearing. He spotted the creature and immediately yelled to his two companions at the top of his voice, "Quickly, run to the center of the clearing!"

Kratos rushed toward Teknon while Phil burrowed underground and out of sight. The creature, dragging its hands on the ground for support, trudged steadily toward Kratos and Teknon. As it drew nearer, Teknon finally got a clear view of the attacker.

The hairless creature was reptilian in appearance. Its arms were long and powerful and its head displayed a single horn that hooked upward. When it reached the packs of equipment, the beast bared its large teeth, then used its claws to rip through the packs, spilling most of the remaining dehydrated food on the ground. Kratos and Teknon watched as the creature gorged itself on the food and then looked over at the warriors as if they were the second course of an unfinished meal.

Kratos cocked his arm and released the Hoplon. The shield ricocheted off the creature's head at the base of its horn. Momentarily stunned, the creature recovered quickly and started toward Teknon. Kratos reached for the Hoplon as it returned and quickly engaged the energy mode, which dramatically increased his strength. As the creature approached, Kratos braced himself to spring toward it. The creature stood straight up and raised its arms in the air, preparing to strike.

A millisecond before Kratos jumped at the beast, it disappeared. Kratos and Teknon stood in shock as they watched the beast sink completely into the ground. The warriors hesitated, then peered over the side of the newly formed crater. The creature, almost 20 meters down with no hope of escape, scratched and pounded the walls.

Teknon's eyes were still fixed on the screeching beast when the snow next to his feet began to swirl. He jumped back, only to see Phil emerging from the ground, spinning like a gyroscope.

Kratos shouted to his friend when he finally stopped spinning. "Well done, Phil!" he said, stepping back from the crater. "I wasn't sure how long I could've slowed that thing down. What is it anyway?"

"A seismos," Phil said, brushing the dirt from his jacket. "It's the most dangerous carnivore in the Thumos Region. This one looked pretty hungry. I wager that he could eat three Teknons before even stopping to belch."

"How did he get so close without our noticing?" Kratos asked.

"Even with its size, a seismos still has incredible stalking capabilities," Phil responded. "The wind and snow made detection even more difficult."

Teknon finally started breathing normally again. He looked cautiously over the edge so he could get another look at the frantic creature. "Phil, how did you make that hole so quickly? I just walked over the top of that ground a minute ago."

"In school we called him Phil the Drill," Kratos said, smiling at his longtime friend. "Phil, do you remember that foundation you dug for the engineering lab?"

Phil chuckled. "The institute would've waited two years before funding that project. You and I decided we didn't want to wait that long to start some of our experiments. So, being the impatient, green-blooded Phasko that I am, I 'dug in' so to speak."

Teknon looked at the damage caused by the seismos. Debris from food and equipment littered the clearing. He kicked a broken container as he walked around the crater, his face contorted with frustration and anger as he folded his arms tightly to shield himself from the bitter cold. He was tired, hungry, and starting to lose perspective. *Where's the end to all of this?* he thought, gritting his teeth. *Why do we continue to put ourselves on the line for this Logos thing? What difference does it make? We're going to get wasted if we keep this up. Amachos, kakos, Harpax, footsoldiers, and now a seismos that wants to eat us like a couple of frozen dinners. What's next?*

Teknon could see Kratos talking with Phil and pointing up the side of the mountain. It was now well into the evening, and there was no sign of the mentors.

Teknon walked over to Kratos and interrupted his conversation with Phil. "Hey, Dad, where are the guys?" Teknon shouted over the wind. "Weren't they supposed to be back by now?"

Kratos looked around at the increasing force of the blizzard. His eyes followed the trail that the mentors were supposed to take up the side of the mountain. He looked back at Teknon and spoke, his voice hesitating. "I tried to reach Arti a few minutes ago, but got no response. I was going to mention it, but then the creature attacked."

"Shouldn't we go look for them?" Teknon said. "It's getting colder every minute. They could be in trouble!"

"We can't risk it," Kratos said. "The snow is too heavy and the wind is picking up again. We've got to find shelter soon, or we'll be in danger. Let's grab whatever gear we can salvage. The storm is worsening fast."

"But ... "

"Right now!" Kratos commanded, picking up a container and a ripped backpack. "We need to find another clearing." Then he turned to his friend. "Phil, once we find a spot, you can do your stuff."

A few minutes later, the three team members pushed up a hill against the forceful wind. Snow began falling so heavily that they could barely see each other, and the cold began to penetrate their suits. Kratos motioned for Phil to proceed as they reached an opening in the trees.

When Phil reached the small clearing, his body immediately started to swirl, creating a vortex of snow at first, followed by a constant flow of broken rock that spewed from the ground like a freshly tapped oil well. Teknon and Kratos huddled together as Phil drilled downward, quickly completing his task. Soon, the swirling of stone and silt slowed to a halt. Phil signaled to his friends to join him inside their temporary underground apartment.

Phil had already turned on the infra-illuminator when his companions entered the room through a small opening in the ground. Although Kratos did not seem surprised by the size and precision of Phil's creation, Teknon stood in amazement as he scanned the cavern. The room was 20 meters wide, 20 meters long, and five meters deep. Ten flawless steps led down to the floor of the chamber. Every edge and surface was as smooth as polished marble. Phil had carved three perfectly formed beds out of stone, each attached to a separate wall. A stone table sat in the center of the room, surrounded by stone benches. As he walked toward a bed, shivering, Teknon strained his eyes to read something on the far wall. He rubbed his face to make sure his eyes weren't playing tricks on him. As he drew closer, he saw the words "Three Warriors Slept Here—Kratos, Teknon, and Phileo," which had been elaborately carved into the wall.

Teknon turned to Phil in bewilderment. "How do you do it, Phil? You made all this in less than five minutes. How?"

"It's a bit hard to explain," Phil said, as he used a perfectly carved stone to cover the entrance. "There's a lot of complicated Phaskian physiology involved. My gloves are also important to the process. I could bore you with a lot of technical details. Just know it's what we Phaskos do best. We're just made this way."

Teknon shook his head and returned a restrained smirk. He walked over to one of the beds and unrolled his mat. He lay down and allowed himself to relax for the first time since they started the hike that morning. Teknon looked over to his father, who was talking with Phil again, this time in whispers. Teknon sat up and tried to get his father's attention in a voice much too loud for the cavern.

"Dad, what about the mentors? Aren't we going to do anything? They could be dying out there!"

Kratos looked at Teknon, then at Phil, then back at Teknon. "We'll have to trust Pneuma. He will give them good judgment, strengthen them to use their unique abilities, and protect them. There's nothing more we can do tonight."

"If I know Matty," Phil said, "he'll crack enough jokes to keep them warm from laughing."

Teknon felt cold and tired, as his hunger started to get the best of him. The smooth stone walls around him still retained the deep chill of the surface terrain. He heard his empty stomach rumbling, and his legs ached. Teknon was worn out and irritated.

"I don't get it," Teknon said angrily. "Our best friends are out in that storm, and you two don't seem to give a flip." Teknon stood up. "And what about us? What are we going to eat? That seismos devoured everything we had." Teknon paced back and forth a few times while Kratos and Phil walked over to the table.

Phil melted some snow on a small thermal unit. As it melted, he mixed it with a packet of nela he had stashed in his vest pocket. He poured the mixture into three small metal cups and sat down. Then he spoke to Teknon. "Come and enjoy a drink, Teknon. We've still got a lot to be thankful for, you know."

"Yeah, yeah," Teknon said, with a caustic tinge ringing in his voice. He paused, then sat down with the other two and slowly took a sip.

"Discouraged?" Kratos asked.

"What do *you* think?" As soon as Teknon spoke, he realized that he had stepped over the line with his tone. He had shown disrespect to the person he respected the most.

"I'm sorry, Dad," he said, dropping his head with an exhausted expression. "Didn't mean to talk to you like that. I'm just fed up with all of this. Why are we doing this, anyway? What difference will it make if we get the Logos or not? Why do we want to put our necks on the line to fight a warped-out cyborg like Magos?" Teknon stood up again. "I'm just ... "

"Tired?" asked Kratos.

"Yeah."

"And hungry?" Phil said, without raising his eyes from his cup.

"Starved," Teknon replied. "Right now, I feel like I could eat the seismos instead of the other way around."

"And still concerned about the mentors?" Kratos inquired.

"Of course," Teknon said. "But it's not just that. I'm starting to wonder about this whole CHAMPION Warrior thing. Am I really cut out for this? Is it even possible for me to become a CHAMPION Warrior with all of the mistakes I've made, or that I will make, for that matter?" Teknon sat on the foot of his bed, shoulders lowered and head bowed. "I don't know. I'm just not feeling real good about things."

"It's easy to lose perspective when you're tired or hungry," Phil said. "Combine that with your anxiety over the absence of your mentors, and you've got a formula for discouragement."

"Okay, so I'm discouraged. Don't you guys get discouraged sometimes? Or am I just *too young* to understand stuff like this?"

"Of course we get discouraged," Kratos replied. "And no, you're not too young to understand. It's just that we want to remind you that it's important to deal with your discouragement and to keep focused on the big picture. Like Phil said, it's easy to forget what's really important when difficulties mount up. When that happens, you start losing hope. We have an important mission to accomplish. You don't need to ask yourself over and over about its importance. In your heart, you know why we're here and what we must accomplish for the future of Basileia. Remember what I told you back on Basileia before we left?"

"And that was ... ?"

"As CHAMPION Warriors, we win or lose by the way we choose!" Phil interjected.

"What's that got to do with it, Phil?" Teknon asked.

"It's a CHAMPION Warrior principle," Phil replied. "It means that no matter what occurs, no matter how we feel, we need to remind ourselves that there is hope for accomplishing the ultimate objective. Even when our emotions tell us otherwise, we must stay focused on trusting Pneuma to help us make the right choices so that we can continue to pursue the mission He has given us. If we can manage discouragement in this way when it comes—and believe me, it will come—then we will stand strong and become a valuable part of the solution for Basileia, and ultimately for the rest of the galaxy."

"A lot has happened recently," Kratos chimed in, "and you're starting to see everything through 'negative glasses,' so to speak. Phil and I learned a long time ago that there is only one sure way to break out of a downward cycle like you're in right now."

"What's that?" Teknon asked.

"When the ancient CHAMPION Warriors were in the thick of battle and the odds were mounting up against them, they called upon the Warrior King. They depended on Him to intervene and grant them victory through His strength."

"Who is this Warrior King?" Teknon asked. "You mean some kind of holographic teacher from the Logos?"

"No," Kratos continued, "someone much more personal than that. The Warrior King is the supreme power in the universe, an ever-present, personal Spirit. The CHAMPIONs reverently referred to Him as Pneuma."

"I've heard you say that before. You mean a spirit we can personally relate to?" Teknon asked, suspicion in his voice.

"Yes," Phil said, taking his cue from Kratos. "When someone became a CHAMPION Warrior, they actually united with Pneuma in spirit and in purpose. So, it was only natural for them to talk with the Warrior King just as easily as I'm talking with you right now."

"I know you and Mom have talked with me about Pneuma all my life, but this sounds too bizarre," Teknon said. "Are you saying Pneuma actually spoke to the CHAMPIONs?"

"Well, they may or may not have actually heard an audible voice," Kratos answered. "But Pneuma did speak to their hearts, and He let them know who He was through His documented teachings. He also revealed Himself supernaturally by intervening in their lives and circumstances. Pneuma took care of them and gave them wisdom, direction, and strength to live like CHAMPIONs."

"So," Teknon inquired, "what does all of this have to do with the Logos?"

"The Logos is the ancient record of Pneuma's teachings," Kratos said. "Through the Logos, Pneuma's followers can listen to the CHAMPION instructors teach how to have a personal relationship with Pneuma as well as how to live by His principles."

"Pneuma gives us the strength to overcome discouragement," Phil said. "As His warriors, we triumph over discouragement by relying solely on Him for everything and focusing on His ultimate purpose for Basileia and for our lives. A true CHAMPION seeks to follow Pneuma's direction—nothing more, nothing less, nothing else." Teknon suddenly recalled a mental picture of Tor on his knees, reciting those exact words. He also recalled many occasions he saw his father doing the same.

"So let me get this straight," Teknon said to his father. "You and Phil actually buy into this stuff?"

"You know that I talk to Pneuma every day and listen for His direction," Kratos replied.

"As do I," Phil added.

"Whoa!" Teknon said, staring at his father and Phil like they had consumed large amounts of gleukos. "I think I've heard enough. I wasn't expecting you to get weird and preachy tonight." Teknon looked directly at his father. "I've known for a long time that you believe some pretty strange stuff, but I guess I never really wanted to come to terms with how really extreme it might be. Why don't we just leave the conversation right there for the night. All I said was that I didn't feel so good. But thanks anyway for the pep talk."

Teknon turned, shaking his head, and walked back to his bunk. "I think I'll turn in. Good night." He lay down and tried to get comfortable on his pad, turning his body toward the opposite wall. Before settling in, however, Teknon turned back to the two men at the table and called out, "Wake me if you hear anything from Arti."

"Will do," Kratos replied. "Good night, Son. Don't forget what we talked about tonight."

"Hmmm," Teknon murmured, pretending not to hear his father's final words. He turned over and closed his eyes.

Shortly, the activity and action of the past few hours overtook him and he fell asleep.

* * *

The next morning, Teknon woke up shivering. He pulled his blanket tightly around his neck, trying to stay warm. As his thoughts became more coherent, he wondered, *Why is this room so cold? Why is light shining in my eyes?*

Teknon sat up and looked around. He was alone. The rock that had covered the shelter's opening was moved away. Sun was shining through the opening, revealing a clear day outside. *Why didn't I hear Phil and Dad get out of bed?* he wondered. *If they're just outside, why can't I hear them talking?*

Teknon climbed off of his bunk and walked up the steps. As he cautiously entered the sunlight, his eyes opened wide. The snow, now firm on the ground, revealed imprints of a recent struggle. Small red and green droplets were sprinkled around on the white blanket of ice. *Dad's blood is red. Phil's is green*, he thought.

Teknon's pulse quickened as he walked carefully around the clearing. He wanted desperately to call out for his father, but hesitated for fear of alerting a possible enemy. His stomach muscles wrenched as he noticed something familiar protruding from the snow. He got on his knees and quickly dug around the object. It was the Hoplon!

Teknon tucked the shield, which was out of its harness, under his arm and stumbled back into the cavern. He quickly scanned the room, looking for anything out of place. He saw the metal cups still sitting on the table. He also saw the gear that Phil had put beside his bed. He climbed frantically back to the surface. He couldn't contain himself any longer.

"Dad! Phil! Where are you?" he yelled as soon as he got outside. His voice bounced off the mountain wall and into the valley. No response. He called again. The echoing sound of his voice was like a repeating message telling Teknon something he didn't want to hear. He was alone. All alone. And he didn't know why.

A Job to Finish

Teknon braced his arms on the table and slowly sat
down. He felt lightheaded, and a wave of nausea swept
through his body. Although he could feel the cool surface of
the stone furniture with his hands, the rest of him seemed to
have no sensation. His thoughts were random, but one
thought in particular pounded like a sledgehammer in his
brain. "I'm alone!" he feverishly whispered aloud. "What do I
do now?"

Queasiness overtook him. He bent over and retched violently. A few moments later, he sat up, wiped his mouth on
his sleeve, and looked up again at the light shining through
the entrance. He closed his eyes while gripping the edges of
the table.

Is it possible? he thought. *Could Dad have been captured? Or
even ... ? No, it's not possible. It can't be.* Teknon collected his
thoughts and the nausea subsided. *What about Phil? If someone
attacked him and Dad, why didn't the attackers come after me?*

Teknon stood up again and started pacing back and forth.
Maybe they went above ground this morning. Maybe they were

ambushed by footsoldiers or even by kakos. The enemies wouldn't know to look for me down here, especially since there was so much fresh snow to cover all traces of the cave. Teknon ran his fingers through his hair. *They've got to be alive.* Suddenly another thought gripped him. *I've got to get out of here before Magos sends something else looking for me!*

Teknon put on his backpack and slid the Hoplon under his arm. He ran up the stairs and through the opening, then looked around, wondering which direction to take. The Hoplon seemed cumbersome tucked under his arm, so he slid his forearm inside the sheaths on the underside of the shield. At first he turned down the mountain, back to Northros. *I'll go back to the cave at the beach and wait there.* Then he hesitated. *But if any of the mentors are still alive, I should try to find them up here rather than take the chance they won't come back to Northros.* He turned and looked up the mountain trail. *Yeah, that's the better option.*

Teknon's movements were quick and jerky as he hiked up the path. He became consumed with the goal of survival; he had to get to someone he knew before something else got to him. His breathing was shallow; his heart raced. He tried not to think about what might have happened to his father or the others. He couldn't let the images creep into his thoughts. That was too much. "Just find one of them," he kept saying aloud as he walked.

Just then, Teknon heard a rustle in the brush. It wasn't loud, but it was there. He ran a little, stopped and listened, then ran again. Something was matching his steps, running a parallel course about 10 meters away. Queasy again, Teknon knew that he had to do something quickly to expose his stalker. He sprinted for a few steps, stopped, and then turned in the direction of the noise.

Suddenly, a form leaped from its cover. An amacho, fangs bared, charged Teknon with its head low and claws outstretched. Teknon froze, and for an instant couldn't even feel his legs. But as the growling creature reached for its prey, Teknon gracefully stepped to one side to avoid the lethal tail. He thrust the shield in an upward motion, catching the amacho under the chin. Simultaneously, he slammed the edge of his foot against the amacho's lower leg. The amacho's head jerked up as its leg bone snapped. The amacho fell on its side, roaring in pain.

Teknon's jaw dropped. He was amazed at his composure as he instinctively positioned his body in an amuno fighting stance. Although injured, the amacho prepared to attack Teknon again. It lunged for Teknon's face with its claws, but the youth carefully leveraged one of the creature's arms and flipped it onto its back. The amacho looked up just in time to see Teknon's forearm thrust the shield into the middle of its chest.

The impact of Teknon's blow caused the air in the amacho's lungs to explode out of its grisly mouth. Beaten, the creature grasped the ground and pushed itself upright again. But just as it stood to its feet, Teknon swung his leg in a perfect half moon, connecting squarely on the shaggy chin of his opponent. The amacho's feet came out from under it, and the beast hit the ground with a thud.

Enthusiasm and confidence pulsed through Teknon like static electricity. He waited a few minutes to see if the amacho would try again, but the creature lay limp on the ground, still and unconscious. He took a final gratifying glance at his conquered opponent and resumed the hike up the mountain trail.

After several minutes, Teknon noticed a nearby clearing that overlooked the valley. He walked over to it and sat down on a large rock. The biting wind reddened his cheeks, but a clear, cold sky replaced the vicious snow and wind that had hammered him and his companions the day before. Northros, bathing in the morning sun, seemed tiny at this distance, and the pleasant time he'd had there seemed a world away.

Teknon sat on the rock for several minutes, thinking about the amacho. The long hours of training in the simulator had prepared him to react quickly to the attack. He felt gratified that the amuno techniques he had learned from his father and mentors were becoming a part of his defense. The rigorous training he had undergone actually made sense for the first time.

Suddenly, he sat up straight. A new perspective hit him square between the eyes. *Wait a minute*, he said angrily to himself. *Wait just a minute!*

As he continued to ponder, Teknon's thoughts took a different direction. *What am I doing? I've got a job to finish. That's why I came here in the first place. Dad said, "As a CHAMPION Warrior, you win or lose by the way you choose!" I'll do my best to find my father and the mentors. But if they were here, they would tell me to focus on the mission of retrieving the Logos. I can't waste time trying to find someone to rescue me.* Teknon thought a few minutes longer. Then the youth paused and looked up at the sky, and did something he had never felt the need to do before.

"Pneuma," he said loudly, "this is Teknon. Dad has told me for a long time that You're more than an idea or cosmic force. I hope You are because I really need You now." Teknon stood up and looked over the beautiful creation across the valley. "I know I've made a lot of mistakes here—and at home. I'm sorry for the ways I've messed up in the past when I have tried to direct my own life. But now I need to complete this mission—Your mission. I don't know where my father and friends are, but I ask You to watch over them. I also ask You to give me the wisdom and strength to pick up where they left off. Help me to get the Logos back. I have a feeling You helped me to take out that amacho. If You can do that, You can strengthen me do whatever it takes to complete this mission. I guess what I'm saying is that from now on, I'm going to depend on You. I will commit my life to You as my father has. Pneuma, please use me and enable me to make the right choices as I finish the job You have given me."

Teknon felt strange talking to someone he couldn't see, but at the same time, a sense of peace and contentment flooded over him. He knew somehow that Pneuma was real and very close to him. Teknon turned and looked up the trail. "Now," he said with resolve, "let's get on with it!"

Teknon walked up the trail for the remainder of the afternoon. It had been more than a day since he had eaten, and he was feeling fatigued. At dusk he reached a small tavern nestled snugly in a crevasse of the mountain. Teknon reached into the lining of his jacket and winced as he remembered that his money had fallen out and scattered in the snow when the seismos attacked. Now he was not only famished, but broke as well.

He pushed open the swinging doors and walked inside. The smoky room contained a bar and several small tables, all filled with customers except one. Conversation was lively as gleukos flowed from dark wooden barrels into large, brimming mugs. No one paid any attention to the hungry boy as he stumbled to a vacant table. He breathed a sigh of relief as he carefully sat down on a well-worn chair that was covered with animal fur. He looked around at the other tables, wondering if any of the customers had seen his companions. A large, powerful-looking woman walked over to Teknon's table and glanced down. "What'll you have, lad?"

"Nothing, ma'am," Teknon said humbly. "I don't have any money. I lost it all on the trail when my dad and I were attacked by a seismos. I just wanted to come in from the cold and rest for a while. I hope you don't mind."

An unexpectedly warm expression flashed over the rugged face of the hostess. "Lost your money, eh?" she replied. "Seems I've heard that one before."

"I'm sure you have," Teknon said, standing up. "But it's true," he said to the woman. "Well, I won't take your table space any longer. Thanks anyway."

Teknon felt her strong, thick hand push him back into the seat. "Where's your father now?" she asked.

"He disappeared on the trail," Teknon responded. "I think he may be in trouble. You haven't seen a man with thick brown hair and a beard, wearing an outfit like mine, have you?"

"Can't say that I have." The woman paused for a moment, and then spoke. "But you look a bit famished, lad. How about a bowl of stew and some sponge toast, on the house?"

"Ma'am?" Teknon said, surprised.

"Would you like some *food*?" she said with emphasis. "You seem like a genuine young fellow. Not unlike my son, rest his soul."

Teknon suddenly felt compassion toward the woman after learning of her son's death. In some ways, the woman's kindness reminded him of his own mother, whom he missed a great deal at this moment. "I'm sorry to hear about your boy," Teknon said. "Thank you for your kindness. I'd really appreciate some food. I haven't eaten since yesterday and I'm about to waste away."

"Name's Trophos, Lady Trophos. I'll be back in a minute with your food." She walked back to the kitchen. "Believe it or not," she said, looking back and smiling, "today's special is seismos stew. It'll be your chance to get even."

Teknon looked around the room as he waited for his meal. Several hunters ate voraciously at the adjoining table. Teknon scratched his neck, trying to identify why he felt strange. It was as if there was a familiar presence nearby, but he couldn't identify what or who it was. The unpleasant sensation gave him a shiver, and he rubbed his hands briskly over his arms.

Lady Trophos soon returned with a huge bowl of steaming soup and a basket of fresh-baked sponge toast. Teknon thanked his new friend several times, then ate so fast that he barely tasted the first few bites. Two liters of soup and a loaf of sponge toast later, Teknon leaned back in his chair and breathed a sigh of contentment. His stomach was full and he was feeling better.

"Lady Trophos," Teknon said as he walked up to the bar, "that was the best meal I've had in a long time. Thanks again."

Lady Trophos beamed as she put a freshly dried glass under the counter. "Glad you liked it, lad."

"I'd better get back on the trail," Teknon said. "But I won't forget you or your kindness."

"It's getting dark out there," she replied. "You sure you won't stay the night? I've got a vacant room I'd be glad to give you."

"No, but thank you," Teknon said gratefully. "I've got to keep going."

"What'll I tell your father if I see him?" she asked, placing both hands on the bar.

Teknon looked at her intently. "Tell him that Teknon went ahead to finish the job."

"I'll do that, Teknon," Lady Trophos replied. "But be careful out there, boy. Don't let nothin' sneak up on you. I'm sure your father would miss his son as much as I miss my own, if something were to happen."

"I'll keep a sharp eye, Lady Trophos," Teknon said, smiling as he placed his right hand on hers. Then he left through the swinging doors.

Teknon walked only a few hundred meters up the trail before the strange feeling of being stalked hit him again. He stopped and turned around. He saw nothing. Strong emotions brewed inside him. His facial muscles tightened; his lips pursed. He no longer feared whatever was waiting for him in the darkness, and he wasn't going to tolerate being stalked.

"All right, show yourself!" Teknon shouted angrily into the darkening countryside. "If you want me, have the courage to face me."

Teknon saw a form enter the path. The light from the tavern shone behind the figure, revealing a tall, human silhouette. The man stopped and faced Teknon.

"Well," Teknon stated, "are you friend or foe?"

"Most definitely foe!" the man replied.

Adrenaline shot through Teknon as he recognized the voice. "Rhegma!" Teknon said, his fists beginning to clench. "Is that you?"

"Indeed, small one," Rhegma replied, his smirking face becoming clear in the moonlight. "I told you back in Bia that we would have another day to continue our conversation and *this* is the day."

"How did you end up here?" Teknon asked as he silently slipped into the amuno stance.

"I had a change of employer," the Harpax replied. "I'm sure you realize that you're a commodity in very high demand."

"Magos?" Teknon asked.

"The same," Rhegma said. "I met my new master soon after you left with your father, who, by the way, no longer appears to be around to protect you."

"What did Magos offer you?" Teknon asked.

"The same as you, young warrior," Rhegma answered

sarcastically. "He offered me immortality. But I understand that you unwisely refused the same offer."

"Magos' definition of immortality and mine are very different," Teknon said. "It's not what it appears, Rhegma."

"Oh, I think it is," Rhegma responded slyly, as he positioned his body to attack. "However, that's not the issue at hand. I've been commissioned to deliver one small, meek, and overcautious house pet to my master. And, by the way, did I mention that means dead or alive?"

"Which is your first choice?" Teknon quipped.

"Actually," Rhegma continued, "the dead option was my idea. Magos wanted to hold you hostage. But when he hears about our violent struggle, and how you refused to be taken alive, well ... "

"After what I saw in Bia, I'm sure that you'll make the process as slow and agonizing as possible, won't you?" Teknon said, continuing to banter.

"Let me put it to you this way," Rhegma said, his knees bending to pounce, "if you have some painkillers stashed in your vest, take them now because this is really going to hurt."

As Teknon prepared himself mentally for battle, he suddenly noticed a strange tingling throughout his body that felt as if someone had injected him with a large dosage of turbocharged adrenaline. A split second later, Rhegma sprang at his prey with a ghastly expression of vengeance.

Teknon was already in his amuno stance when Rhegma smashed, face-first, into what appeared to be an invisible wall. The Harpax fell to the ground, gripping his face in pain. For a moment, Teknon stood motionless, astonished by what he had seen. Then it hit him. He glanced down at the circular object attached to his forearm.

The Hoplon is working! he thought. *How, I don't know, but Rhegma just slammed into the force field!*

Rhegma grimaced and moaned as he tried to stand up. Teknon's mind raced as he tried to remember what his father had said about using the Hoplon. Dad said that the Hoplon worked on brain commands. He also said he could only use one mode at a time. Teknon gritted his teeth and tried to focus all of his concentration in one direction: increasing his strength.

The process took only a few seconds, but Teknon was vividly aware of every sensation. It started in his fingers and toes. A warmth, almost like the feeling of sunlight, surged over his skin and through his limbs. His uniform felt tight around the shoulders and chest as his muscle structure expanded slightly. He felt the fiber in his frame hardening, until finally his entire body felt like a metallic extension of the shield. Teknon felt exhilarated, energized, and very, very strong.

Teknon leaned down and grasped Rhegma by his jacket. Rhegma slammed his fist onto Teknon's arm in hopes of breaking the youth's grip. Instead, Teknon's arm absorbed the Harpax's blow like a carbonic beam, and Rhegma drew his hand back in pain. Teknon was still adjusting to his enhanced power when he raised Rhegma above his head and nearly launched him into the air. The Harpax felt like a blade of grass in his hand.

Rhegma looked down on his overpowering opponent in shock. "What's going on here?" he shouted. "How is this possible?"

"What was that you said about needing *painkillers*, Rhegma?" Teknon replied, confidently. "I think I still have a few here in my vest, if you're interested."

"Put me down, you miniature wartmouse!" Rhegma continued, this time with panic in his voice.

Teknon cocked his arm and threw Rhegma against a nearby tree. The huge Harpax hit the wooden surface hard. The impact snapped his arm above the elbow, and blood poured out from his forehead. He cringed as he saw Teknon approaching, this time with the tavern's light at his back. His well-defined silhouette revealed the outline of the Hoplon.

Teknon spoke in a tone that caused the Harpax to cower even more. "Let me put it to you straight, Rhegma," he said. "I've got a mission to complete, and not you or any other of Magos' puppets are going to prevent me from accomplishing it. Now, you can give me the information I need, or I'll transform you into a casualty of war. What'll it be?"

"You can't possibly get the Logos by yourself," Rhegma sneered. "You're the one who will become a casualty."

"Let me worry about that," Teknon replied. He looked around until he spotted the right tool of persuasion. Then he used one hand to grasp a log the size of a hovercraft and effortlessly raised it over his head. Rhegma's hands covered his face.

"Last chance, Harpax," Teknon said firmly. "Tell me the location of the fortress, or I'll give you a headache that painkillers won't touch."

Rhegma pointed due south. "It's over that ridge, through the Thumos Forest. It will take at least a week by foot. If the cold doesn't get you, a pack of amachos will. You'll never make it."

Teknon threw the log at least 10 meters into the brush. "I don't think that's going to be a problem, Rhegma," he said, as he looked toward the south. Then he faced his groveling opponent. "I suggest that you rethink your commitment to this master of yours," Teknon barked. "Whether you believe it or not, Magos isn't able to give you what you're looking for. He'll transform and control you just like he has his other goons. The only way you're going to find long-lasting satisfaction is to change masters and turn your life around. You probably won't listen to me now, but you should consider what the CHAMPION Warriors have to say about living. Come and listen to the Logos when I get it back. You won't be sorry."

Rhegma gritted his teeth. "Either kill me or leave me, boy. But don't insult me with your preaching."

"I'm off then," Teknon said. "Don't try this again, Rhegma. And think about what I said." With that, Teknon left his angry and injured attacker in the evening snow.

As soon as Teknon was out of Rhegma's sight, he looked for the nearest clearing and stopped. Once again he looked at the tool on his arm that had served him so effectively against Rhegma. *Well*, Teknon thought, *this thing's worked so far. Let's see if it can help me take the bird's-eye route to Magos' fortress.*

Teknon placed the Hoplon on the ground and cautiously put one foot on the left side of the shield's surface. His face tightened, and he closed his eyes as he put his other foot on the right side. Teknon considered for a moment what he should think about. Nothing came to mind. All he knew was that he wished he could be flying like his dad did, far above the trees toward the destination. He envisioned himself looking down on the forest, with the frigid air stinging his face as he streaked across the evening sky. There he stood, eyes closed, surrounded by the darkness, trying to balance himself on a round metallic object. He felt silly but continued to think about sailing through the moonlit sky. Nothing happened. After a few more seconds, Teknon sighed deeply and prepared to step off the shield.

He scoffed, "So much for that ... " Sudden movement in the shield interrupted his words. The Hoplon began to separate on both sides, revealing the intricate workings within the shield. Short winglets extended from either side. Braces formed around his feet. Teknon hesitated, then slowly looked toward the sky, resumed his concentration, and envisioned himself going straight up.

Before he could take another breath, Teknon was more than 300 meters above the ground. His stomach felt as if he had left it a hundred of those meters beneath him. He paused, his eyes wide with shock and exhilaration. Slowly, he focused his thoughts on moving in a horizontal direction. In a split second, Teknon saw trees passing beneath him like waves of water. He looked ahead and barely had enough time to imagine going over the mountain ledge in front of him. He tried to think about slowing down, and the Hoplon abruptly stopped. As it hovered leisurely in the sky, Teknon attempted to regain his bearings.

Okay, okay, he thought, trying to calibrate his mental navigation. *I think I'm getting the hang of this.* He faced south and positioned his body like he was about to take his hoverboard down one of the steep slopes of Basileia. The sky was clear and the twin moons lit the countryside with a soft tint of blue. He was ready.

"Next stop, the home of my enemy," he said out loud. The Hoplon responded and soared gracefully across the sky, like a bird of prey.

Teknon covered many kilometers during the next hour. Soon he entered Magos' section of the Thumos Region. He saw a well-defined light shining on the ground a few kilometers away. He reduced his speed and glided in to get a better look. As he drew closer, he blinked his eyes several times to make sure he wasn't hallucinating. He set the Hoplon down slowly, right next to the lighted field, and the braces released his feet.

Teknon was speechless, and his heart raced as he walked toward six individuals, standing in a semicircle, looking as if they had been waiting for his arrival. He tried to talk to them, but words wouldn't come.

"Hello, Son, we've been expecting you," a friendly voice said.

"Dad?" Teknon finally responded, his voice barely audible. Before he could say another word, he noticed that his father was wearing something on his back. Something that shouldn't be there—it was the Hoplon.

EPISODE FOURTEEN

BACK TO BACK

Teknon quickly looked back at his Hoplon, a few feet away. Then he glanced at Kratos again to make sure his father was also wearing a shield. *How can both of us have Hoplons?* He wondered. *Is he really my father? Or is this just an elaborate holographic hallucination cooked up by Magos to prevent me from continuing my mission?* Teknon scanned around the campsite at the friendly faces waiting for him, ready to grab his Hoplon in defense if needed.

"Before your palms get any clammier," Kratos said, "let me assure you that you are using your very own shield." Kratos put his hands on Teknon's shoulders, and then warmly embraced him. "And by the way, you did very well!"

"But ... " Teknon started to respond.

"Nice bout with the amacho," Tor said, smiling, as his massive hand grasped Teknon by the top of his head and shook it playfully.

Matty walked over and slapped his young companion on the back. "Great line with Rhegma about giving him 'a headache painkillers won't touch.'"

Teknon was still gathering his thoughts as Epps, Arti, and Phil also welcomed him. As the greetings subsided, Teknon finally found the words to start his questioning. "What are you guys doing here?" Teknon asked. "What happened back at the camp? From the looks of things, I thought you'd been ambushed."

"Your father and I created the look of disaster at the camp," Phil responded.

"And the red and green spots on the ground?" Teknon asked.

"Camouflage coloring," Kratos said. "We wanted you to think that Phil and I had been hurt."

"Well, believe me, it worked," Teknon said, his face flushing in anger. "But how did you know about the amacho and Rhegma? What were you doing, hiding in the woods watching me suffer?"

Arti held up his Sensatron and walked over to Teknon. The mentor reached carefully under Teknon's left arm and pulled off what looked like a spot of dirt from his clothing. Then Arti pointed to a blip on the screen of the Sensatron, revealing the location of the small tracking device removed from Teknon's clothing.

"Not only did we know your location," Arti said, "we could hear your conversations through a tiny microphone on the tracking device. "We were also able to monitor your heart rate as well as the rest of your vital signs. We knew everything you were doing."

Epps jumped into the conversation. "We even knew when you met our primary operative in the Thumos Region."

"Who was that?" Teknon asked. Then a thought came to his mind before Epps could respond. "You don't mean Lady Trophos?"

"That's right," Kratos responded grinning. "Phil and I met her years ago at the institute. She's a dear friend and a brilliant engineer. She's also one of the bravest and most loyal followers of the CHAMPION movement."

"What was she doing at the tavern?" Teknon asked. "She acted liked she owned the place."

"She does," Phil replied. "A few years ago, she agreed to come to the Thumos Mountains and purchase the tavern to use as an information base. She's been living there and gathering important data about Magos and his fortress ever since. Sounds like she took a real liking to you."

"So this was all a setup?" Teknon said, clenching his teeth. "Do you have any idea what went through my mind during the past day and a half? I had to deal with the idea that my father and my closest friends were probably dead! I didn't know where you were or what had happened. I didn't think I would even make it *this* far!"

"But you did," Epps said proudly.

"I was willing to do whatever I had to do to get that Logos back because I thought it was the right thing to do," Teknon continued.

"We know, pal," Matty said.

"I could've been killed!" Teknon exclaimed, bewildered by his companions' responses.

"But you weren't," Kratos said. "Pneuma protected you, didn't He?"

"You heard that, too?" Teknon said. He paused for a moment, his head shaking. "Well, I guess that stuff you and Phil said about spiritual guidance and strength started making sense after all." Then Teknon looked directly at his father. "But why did you leave me out there? With everything we have to face ahead with Magos, why did you take the time and energy to put me through an obstacle course like that?"

"Two reasons," Kratos replied. "First, you came on this mission because I asked you. During the course of our journey, you've learned a lot about the CHAMPIONs and our mission. But until now, you didn't own our mission."

"Own the mission?" Teknon asked.

"You hadn't made it yours," Tor injected. "You gained the head knowledge about becoming a CHAMPION, but not the conviction of heart. For that, you had to face the possibility that no one else would retrieve the Logos unless you stepped in. When you did, the mission not only belonged to us, but to you as well."

Teknon pondered as his enormous mentor spoke these words of encouragement. Then he looked at his father. "And what was the second reason?"

"So that you would fully understand that Pneuma is the ultimate source of your strength and protection," Kratos replied in a serious tone. "In the course of your struggle, you realized your need for Him. Pneuma was all that you needed to succeed. But you couldn't realize He was all you needed until He was all you had. And when He was all you had, then you realized He was all that you needed."

"In other words," Teknon said. "I didn't know who was really in charge around here until now!"

"I think the boy's got it!" Matty said.

"Now, for your final answer," Kratos said, while the other team members began smiling and nodding at each other.

"Answer? What's the question?" Teknon said. Kratos pointed to the shield lying on the ground behind his son. "Oh, yeah!" Teknon exclaimed, remembering his initial thought when he entered the camp. He ran back to the weapon and picked it up.

"This thing worked for me!" Teknon said. Kratos nodded. Then Teknon pointed to the circular device on his father's back. "But what's that doing there if I've got this one here? I thought there was only one Hoplon."

"Well, there's only one that belongs to me," Kratos said, smiling.

"Are you saying what I think you're saying?" Teknon said excitedly.

"I created two Hoplons," Kratos responded. "One shield that would respond to me, and another that would respond to my son when he had attained the focus and maturity required to use it. I transported the second shield to Lady Trophos before we came to Kairos. She delivered it to me the night we stayed in the underground room while you slept. Tell me, Teknon, has my son reached the point where he is ready to carry the shield of a CHAMPION Warrior?"

"You bet he has!" Teknon yelled. Holding his shield in front of him, he walked over to his companions with his new trophy. They congratulated him as he proudly placed the shield back on his arm.

Kratos walked over to the rest of the group. He stroked his beard while he talked. "There is one thing I must mention to you about your Hoplon."

"What's that?" Teknon asked.

"The Hoplon is yours for the time being. If we are successful in completing our mission," Kratos replied, "I may ask you to return your shield to me. Will you be willing to do that?"

"I guess so, Dad," Teknon said, a little confused and disappointed. "If that's what you want."

"I have reasons for making such a request, but there's no need to think about them now," Kratos said. "You'll be able to use your Hoplon sooner than you think. In fact, gentlemen," Kratos said, looking around, "I think we should take a short rest now and then go over our plans for tomorrow." He pointed to the big fellow. "Tor, you take the first watch."

"What happens tomorrow?" Teknon asked.

"Tomorrow," Tor said firmly, as he moved into position to guard the camp, "we complete our mission!"

Although he had gone for a long time without sleep, Teknon could not close his eyes. His hand lay lightly on top of his Hoplon as he looked into the starlit sky with a new feeling of belonging to this team and this mission. Although Teknon knew that the battle ahead would be real and dangerous, the thought of it didn't arouse the fear that he anticipated. He no longer felt alone. He had his father, his friends, and now the Warrior King to guide him. Whatever outcome awaited him, Teknon knew that he was doing the right thing. And with Pneuma's help and direction, he felt ready for the task.

A few hours later, the team gathered around a small clearing in the lighted field. Kratos projected a holographic image of Sheol from his Hoplon, then he walked over to the three-dimensional image of the fortress and pointed to its perimeter. "The fortress is 10 kilometers due south of here," Kratos described. "We estimate that approximately 50 footsoldiers guard the border of Sheol. We've got to get past them to get inside the tower. But first we've got to get Arti close enough to disengage the energy field with his Sensatron."

"How can he do that?" Teknon inquired.

"Fortunately, the field is composed of the same type of energy created by your shields rather than the tantronic energy Scandalon used to trap us," Arti replied. "Since we know how the Hoplon is designed, we can program a de-energizing force to neutralize the energy field."

"How are we going to divide the team to enter fortress?" Tor asked.

"Matty and I will try to reach Magos in his chamber," Kratos replied. "The rest of you will find the Logos. Lady Trophos said that it's in a huge room behind a massive armored door." Kratos looked intently at Teknon. "And don't forget about Dolios. He'll be guarding the Logos."

"Why are you and Matty splitting out from the rest of us?" Teknon asked, concern rising in his voice.

"We need to utilize the best mix of our skills to produce the greatest results," Epps interjected.

"Besides," Matty said confidently, "I want my shot at that senile cyborg. I'll run so many circles around Magos his sensors will short-circuit."

Kratos asked, "Mat, have you got the adhesive?"

"Adhesive?" Teknon asked.

"Just a precaution," Kratos replied. Then he turned to the rest of the mentors. "Remember, gentlemen," Kratos continued, "with Magos you must expect the unexpected. He knows we're coming, so he'll be waiting for us to attack. Take nothing for granted. I'm not sure how much he knows about our skills or our weaponry, but I do know that he cannot comprehend the level of our conviction or the depth of our relationship with Pneuma. That is our greatest advantage."

"We must function at all times as a team," Tor added. "We have learned to eat, sleep, and fight like a team. Remember that there is great power in a team. Now we must show this author of evil what great power we have." Tor turned and growled a few more words as he continued to prepare for departure. "Besides, Magos doesn't realize that real CHAMPION Warriors love the thrill of battle."

Matty grinned as he turned to Teknon and pointed at Tor. "The big guy really gets into this stuff, doesn't he?"

Both Kratos and Teknon placed their shields on the ground and waited as their feet became fixed in place. Matty walked around like a professional athlete, stretching his well-toned legs. Tor continued to grin with anticipation as he adjusted his arm braces. Epps flexed his fingers as his gloves expanded into position. Arti glanced again at his Sensatron before closing its top and attaching the unit to his belt. Phil popped several energy bars into his mouth as he looked across the mountainside.

"Watch each other's backs," Kratos said, looking fondly at his companions. "Remember what I told you when we left Basileia. No man is worthy who is not ready at all times to risk body, status, and life itself for a great cause."

"For His honor and glory!" Tor yelled.

"For His honor and glory!" the rest shouted in unison.

Within moments, the seven figures vanished from the lighted field. They moved like a synchronized unit through the darkness, fast on its way to the menacing towers of Sheol. Kratos and Teknon streaked side by side on their Hoplons across the sky. In a matter of minutes, explosive beams of energy shot out from the towers and flashed past them on either side. Kratos and Teknon decreased their altitude and darted back and forth to dodge the deadly beams.

On the ground, Matty matched the airborne warriors' speed. Because of his swiftness and enhanced agility, he was able to prevent his feet from triggering hidden explosive devices. Tor, Arti, and Epps, on the other hand, ran as fast as they could on a direct line toward the first perimeter. Phil carefully and precisely drilled beneath the surface, trying to locate buried mines. His vast experience in traveling through various textures of soil and rock gave him the ability to sense buried objects long before he or his companions reached them.

The middle tower of Magos' stronghold soon came into view. Arti glanced at the Sensatron, hoping to neutralize the energy field as soon as possible. Suddenly a large robotic fist pierced through the darkness and caught Arti across the chin.

The footsoldier rushed toward the stunned warrior, preparing to finish him off. Arti, recovering quickly, waited until the footsoldier was within striking distance, then thrust the heel of his boot directly into his attacker's chest. Wires snapped, sparks flew, and the footsoldier slammed into the ground. Arti cocked his arms behind his head, braced them against the ground, and thrust himself upward into an amuno stance.

Twenty footsoldiers charged the trio from all sides. Tor immediately thrust his fists forward and fired a burst of energy beams from his braces. In an instant, ten of the hulking androids found themselves surrounded and bound like a bundle of firewood. Tor swung the lassoed footsoldiers around until sufficient speed allowed the huge mentor to throw his opponents far into the distance.

Epps delivered focused blows to several footsoldiers. He followed his punches with piercing leg strikes, delivering them with the fluid accuracy of an amuno master.

As the last footsoldier within his reach slammed to the ground, Epps turned toward Arti and shouted, "Arti, disable the field!"

Arti delivered a crushing blow to a footsoldier, forcing him back into several other androids. Then he looked at the Sensatron and punched in the appropriate code. Unfortunately, he didn't see two other footsoldiers sneaking up from behind. Teknon's shield connected with one of the androids, then careened off the head of the other before returning to its new owner more than 20 meters away.

"Nice throw, Teknon!" Arti shouted as he quickly finished programming the Sensatron. A shining red light indicated that his job had been accomplished. "The field is down!" he yelled.

"Nice goin', Ace!" Matty shouted to Arti as he turned and waved to his leader. "Kratos! Let's go!"

"All right," Phil said to his companions as he emerged from a pit, leaving 30 footsoldiers helpless to escape, "shall we continue?"

"Proceed, maestro," Epps replied.

Before burrowing beneath the surface again, Phil looked at his young teammate. "Ready, Teknon?"

"As Tor would say," Teknon shouted, while dropping his shield to the ground, "I'm ready to roll 'em!" Within seconds, he shot into the air like a missile.

As Teknon reached cruising altitude his father waved a confident farewell to him. For a brief moment, the two shared a glance of love and admiration. Then Kratos banked his shield to the left and streaked toward the upper level of the middle tower. Teknon lingered a moment as he watched his father soar through the glaring spotlights of Sheol. Then the young warrior turned and followed his other companions on their alternate course.

Kratos saw Matty bolt ahead just before they reached the tower. The speedster darted up the side of the tall structure, his footgear clinging effectively. Kratos reached the lookout point in Magos' chamber, where he hovered and waited for Matty to arrive. Then, without warning, Kratos began to fall from the air. He tried unsuccessfully to reengage the Hoplon's flight mode. Matty looked up just in time to see his leader plummeting toward him.

Matty braced himself as he reached up and caught Kratos in mid-stride. The Hoplon was still attached to Kratos as Matty ran up the wall and reached the ledge of Magos' chamber. Matty supported Kratos as he stepped onto the ledge. Kratos looked up at Matty as he manually detached his feet from the shield and folded it into the harness.

"What happened?" Matty asked quietly. "All of the sudden you started falling like a sack of stone biscuits."

"We must have passed through a second energy field, one designed to disable our weapons," Kratos replied, whispering.

"But why didn't I fall with you?" Matty pursued. "I use the same technology you do."

Kratos thought a moment. "Not quite, Matty. Your suit and shoes interact with your body chemistry as well as with your brain waves. You may be the only one of us who'll be able to function at full capacity."

"No worries, Captain," Matty said with a smirk. "I'll rise to the occasion."

Kratos carefully peeked around the corner of the ledge and

into Magos' chambers. "Let's keep it quiet. I'm not sure when we're going to run into the digital dictator."

*   *   *

Teknon groaned as he slowly sat up. He pulled his feet from the Hoplon and shook his head. He felt Tor grasp his underarm and pull him to his feet.

"You're lucky you were flying so close to the ground," Tor said. "I guess we didn't give you enough time to get used to flying that thing."

"Unfortunately," Arti said, glancing at the Sensatron, "it's not Teknon's aeronautical ability that's in question. It's our weapons."

"What?" Epps said, examining his gloves. "Have our weapons malfunctioned?"

Tor's face grimaced as he attempted to engage his arm braces. "Nothing," he said. "Not even a flicker. We will have to face our foes unarmed, at least for the moment."

Arti looked intently at the Sensatron and frowned. "It will be more than a moment, my friend. Our weapons have been completely disabled by an alternate energy field. From now on, we'll have to rely exclusively on our amuno abilities."

"At least I'm not hampered," Phil said with reassurance. "I suggest we find the room with the armored door as quickly as possible."

The five warriors cautiously entered the main entrance of the middle tower, constantly looking for footsoldiers and kakos that might ambush them. They passed through the wide halls of the elaborate structure, glancing occasionally at control panels that flashed and beeped on either side of them. They could not understand why they were able to advance toward the Logos unhindered.

"I don't like this," Tor grumbled. "Why haven't we been attacked? I'd prefer a head-on collision rather than this vile waiting."

"Patience, big fellow," Arti said in a low tone. He glanced at the Sensatron. "I'm getting fibronic readings. Something is coming closer. I suggest ... " Before Arti could finish his sentence, something else on the screen of his instrument caught his eye. "Back to back, quickly!"

Before the warriors could react, 2 five-meter high, transparent panels slammed down on either side of them, filling the hall from floor to ceiling and encasing the team. A moment later, a dozen footsoldiers and two kakos filled the hall on either side of the panels. Tor immediately lowered his shoulder and slammed his massive body into one of the panels. The force of Tor's impact shook the floor, but the panel remained intact.

Teknon looked on either side of the cage, feeling like a captured animal about to be sacrificed. He thought he heard something strange and looked up in the direction of the noise. Several vents opened, and a blue-colored gas began spewing down on its way toward the team members. "It's highly toxic—get down!" Arti yelled. "If we inhale it, our respiratory systems will shut down in seconds."

Phil hurriedly scanned the floor and spoke to Arti. "What's the composition of these panels?"

"It's some sort of transparent carbonic alloy," Arti answered. "There's no way we can penetrate it."

"How about the floor?" Phil inquired.

"Basic granitine compound. Similar to the rock found outside."

"Sounds like your cup of nela, Phil," Teknon said anxiously.

Are you ready, gentlemen?" Phil said quietly.

"Let's roll 'em!" Tor said.

Phil's body instantly converted into his solidified, altered state. He began spinning so fast that his body resembled a whirling cloud of dust. He dove headfirst into the floor, creating an opening large enough for the entire team. The evil androids stared with an emotionless gaze at the empty containment field as the sound of grinding rock filled the room behind them.

The kakos were first to turn and see the five figures in fighting stances, ready for battle. Tor jumped high and long toward his opponents, striking several footsoldiers before landing with perfect balance. A footsoldier opened his chest panel and shot a cable toward Arti, but the nimble warrior ducked under the piercing metallic rope. At the same time, Arti lunged forward to deliver a severing snap kick to the shin of his attacker. The android fell to the ground, his leg detached from his robotic body. Phil began spinning again, this time hurtling large chunks of the granitine floor toward the androids. Footsoldiers and kakos alike flew backward as the pieces of rock hit them like cannon shots.

Teknon took his Hoplon from its harness and prepared to throw it, even though he knew it would not return. After throwing his shield, Teknon planned to do whatever damage he could to the first android he could reach. As he cocked his arm, Epps grabbed his arm. No, Teknon!" Epps said sternly. "Find the Logos. We will take care of these creatures and join you when we can. You must go!"

"But ... " Teknon said, lowering the shield.

"Go, Teknon, now!" Tor shouted, crashing the heads of two footsoldiers together.

Teknon ran toward the open end of the hallway, looking quickly down every branching hall for the armored door. His body was bursting with energy, and he was running faster than he could ever remember. He hated leaving his friends but was determined to reach the target. As he rounded a corner, a familiar figure stood calmly in his path: Scandalon. The android seemed to be waiting for Teknon.

Teknon instantly recognized Scandalon from their encounter outside of the mining village. Teknon reflexively reached for his arm and slid his fingers over the scar he had received from Scandalon. Anger began rising inside of him. He prepared to jump at the motionless android but hesitated. *I have a bigger objective to accomplish than defeating Scandalon,* Teknon thought. *This mindless servant is merely an obstacle I must overcome in order to complete this mission.*

Teknon also remembered what his father had emphasized about amuno. Kratos said that their ancient fighting style was most effective when the opponent made the first move. *Last time, I struck first,* Teknon thought. *Let's see if an android can get impatient.*

Several moments passed, but they felt like hours. Neither Scandalon nor Teknon moved an inch.

All right, Teknon whispered to himself, *what are the options?* He quickly looked around the room. *Is there anything I could use to overcome his first move?*

Suddenly Scandalon's arm began to change into a deadly razor-sharp shape. Teknon calmly positioned his body in anticipation. When the blade shot forward, like a penetrating missile, Teknon dodged it. At the same time he raised the Hoplon to face level, and deflected the blade as it passed into one of the computer panels on the wall. Scandalon's piercing weapon entered the panel with a sound of tearing metal. A small explosion almost knocked Teknon off his feet as a current of energy flashed back across the android's silvery extension to its source. Scandalon's robotic body lifted off the ground as the hot gases of his vaporized internal structure expanded rapidly. Moments later, he exploded like a balloon overfilled with air. Teknon was barely able to dodge the fragments of Scandalon's mechanized body that flew past him.

Teknon stepped over the scattered remains of his devilish adversary, enjoying the exhilaration of defeating the foe that had caused him so much difficulty. He continued his search, but didn't go far before he was standing in front of an ominous, metallic entrance. *Beyond this door*, Teknon thought, *is the object of our mission. Now I have to get inside.*

*   *   *

Several hundred meters above Teknon and his companions, Kratos and Matty searched for the evil master of Sheol. Kratos knew that in order for Basileia to be free from the threat of moral decay and perversion, they must find a way to stop Magos. Although retrieving the Logos was very important, Kratos knew that Magos would never be satisfied until he succeeded in manipulating the minds of Basileians so that one day they would do his will. With his shield functioning at minimal capacity, however, Kratos felt vulnerable and less capable of defeating his old partner. But he knew he had to try.

Matty walked in front of Kratos as they entered an enormous, darkened room filled with complex video screens and panels of digital equipment that displayed various forms of data. The muscles in Kratos' face tightened as he looked up at one of the larger video screens. It was divided into six sections. Images of Tor, Epps, Arti, and Matty surrounded life-size pictures of Teknon and himself.

Matty was only a few meters ahead of Kratos when two panels suddenly descended, enclosing the swift mentor in a transparent trap. Matty pushed on both panels, but could not break out. Kratos also tried to crack the clear wall on his side of the enclosure by slamming the Hoplon against it. As light began to radiate from several corners of the room, a door slid open with a sound like someone running his fingers over the strings of an electronic harp. Kratos glanced up at the balcony that overlooked the room and tried to keep his composure as a throne carrying a familiar figure emerged from the door, floating forward to the edge of the balcony.

Magos stood up slowly and deliberately. The towering cyborg sneered at his captives. Kratos projected a calm image to Magos, but inside he was thinking through his options as fast as possible. "So you have finally come to me, my old friend," Magos said, his voice sounding like it was being filtered through a digital synthesizer. "If you remember, I told you this day would come."

"You know why I'm here, Magos," Kratos replied.

"Yes, I suppose I do," Magos replied. "But that objective is only a temporary obstacle that I will help you to overcome. You see, Kratos, your destiny is here with me in Sheol." Magos strode with a long, powerful gait across the balcony. "I am going to conquer this galaxy, and you will help me to do it."

Kratos stood as tall as he could and looked directly into the eyes of his enemy. "You know that isn't possible. I intend to retrieve the Logos. Furthermore, I'm dedicated to preventing you from making further advances toward destroying the moral fiber of Basileia. I'm here to stop you, Magos."

"A pity," Magos replied, sitting down. "And I had so hoped that this would be a less painful process."

Suddenly the antenna on Magos' head began to glow.

Kratos faced Matty's transparent cage as a large piece of equipment descended through an opening in the ceiling. It looked like a powerful gun and it moved around in various directions, as if it were trying to find a target. When it stopped, the barrel of the gun was pointed directly at Matty.

An orange beam shot from the gun, and Matty dodged it at the last millisecond. Another beam shot out, then another, then another. Matty focused intently on the weapon, moving back and forth so quickly that the color of his uniform seemed like a coat of paint on the glass. Magos chuckled. "He's fast, Kratos, but he can't evade the laser forever. Soon he'll vaporize like a cloud of mist. And he's not the only one who will suffer from your decision."

"What do you mean?" Kratos asked, already knowing the answer.

Magos stared directly into Kratos' eyes. "Your friends are, at this moment, facing the force of my army. And as for your young warrior, he will soon perish as he faces his deepest fear. Is this what you want, Kratos?"

"What I *want* is of no consequence," Kratos replied confidently. "What I'll *do* is the right thing—by stopping you!"

Magos reeled around as anger covered his face. Then, he stood up and began pacing with violent zeal. "You still fail to grasp it, don't you, old friend?" Magos said using a low, deliberate tone.

"What do you mean?" Kratos questioned, as his hand slid slowly up his leg toward his jacket.

Magos continued his long unbroken striding. He looked around the room and spoke, as if to himself. "Even now, as you stand on the brink of defeat, you cannot see the scope of all that's before you."

"I don't quite get your meaning, Magos," Kratos responded. He watched Magos closely, waiting for him to turn away long enough so he could make a move.

Suddenly Magos stopped pacing. His powerful arms hung, with fists clenched, at his side as he fixed his frame in a determined stance to face his adversary. His normal eye narrowed. "You still believe that I am the center of all your concerns.

You think it's me, Magos, that stands between you and victory for your home planet."

"Well, don't you?" Kratos asked in earnest.

Magos continued. "I am strong, Kratos. More so than even you realize. But I am but a general in the battle for this universe."

"A general?" Kratos replied. "Whom do you serve?"

"Magos turned slightly and glanced at the various monitors around the room. "Whom?" he said wryly. "*Whom* is such a limiting term." His face displayed an expression of pious arrogance. "Nevertheless, his name is Poneros. Oh, Kratos," Magos said, continuing to gaze around the room, "the sheer power that he possesses. Power beyond belief. You cannot begin to imagine what power and resources might be at your disposal if only you were to gain the vision of what could be."

When Magos momentarily turned his gaze in the opposite direction, Kratos carefully reached inside his jacket. Without warning Magos faced Kratos again. His transocular implant pulsated with light. His voice resonated with fury.

He shouted contemptuously. "But you would refuse all that Poneros could offer, wouldn't you? Very well, CHAMPION. If you will not come to me on your own accord, I will help you to become more willing."

A ray of light shot from Magos' eye implant and into Kratos' face. Kratos froze in place, his eyes fixed on Magos with a paralyzed expression. Magos was using his power to manipulate and transform Kratos' mind. Kratos' hand, immobilized inside of his jacket, could not remove the hidden item.

Realizing that his leader was in imminent danger, Matty stopped his evasive efforts and looked directly into the barrel of the laser. Then he began spinning in place. Faster and faster he went, resembling Phil but moving at a much higher velocity. The laser shot again at Matty, but this time the beam deflected off the thermal barrier created by Matty's spinning. The deflected beam bounced off the transparent panel, then careened into the section of the wall that stood between the two clear panels, creating a small hole. The laser continued its rapid fire, bouncing off Matty again and again. It looked as if a fireworks display was occurring within the panels as beam after beam carved more holes in the far wall; finally, an opening was created that was big enough for him to escape through. Matty stopped his spinning, dodged one more beam, and darted through the hole. Magos was still focusing his transforming power on Kratos, slowly breaking down the warrior's defenses. Kratos knew what was happening but was helpless to stop it.

*　　*　　*

Teknon stood in front of the massive door trying to determine how he could penetrate it. He recoiled when he heard a loud creaking noise, like the sound of large pieces of metal grinding against one another. He stepped back a few paces as the door opened in front of him, then inched forward to gain a glimpse of what was waiting for him on the other side.

Teknon could see little in the blackness. As he crept inside and his eyes adjusted, he began to view a funnel of light in the center of the room. The light encircled a luminous, circular object. Teknon gasped as he came closer.

"The Logos!" he whispered.

Teknon gazed deeply into the small, colorful sphere. It looked like nothing he had ever seen. He felt drawn to it, just as he was drawn to water when he was thirsty. He was overcome with a desire to touch the Logos and reached both hands forward to grasp it. The large metal doors slammed shut behind him, and he heard movement in the other side of the room. He immediately stepped back from the Logos and slid smoothly into a fighting stance.

Teknon scanned the room until he sighted a form that materialized from the darkness. Teknon knew that if something was in the room, it could only mean one thing: Dolios was guarding the Logos. Teknon mentally prepared himself for battle.

When Teknon saw his opponent's face, his eyes widened and he drew a deep breath. It was his father's face! But as Teknon's eyes focused, he could see that something was terribly unfamiliar. This was not the image of the father he knew.

The figure that stood before Teknon was a dark, corrupt-looking version of Kratos. The eyes were narrow and grim, the hair dirty and uncombed, and the expression grinning with a sly expression of evil. Rings adorned his fingers, and earrings gleamed from both ears.

Teknon also noticed that the individual was wearing the clothes of a Harpax. His heart began beating, almost to the breaking point. Seeing the image of his father in this condition caused Teknon to completely lose his concentration. He wanted to run away as fast as he could. Tears started forming in the corner of his eyes, and his legs shook as the figure spoke to him.

"So, you've come to face me, have you?" Dolios said in a condescending manner. "You stupid young fool. Did you really think you had what it takes to complete this mission?"

These words stung Teknon like a thousand needles. The voice was exactly like his father's. Teknon didn't know how to respond. He was still fighting the temptation to acknowledge this image of his father as reality. The image was overpowering to Teknon. *I can't let myself believe this is really my father,* he thought.

*   *   *

Magos felt his opponent's mind transforming with every passing second. The android's grin widened as he sensed that the victory he had so long desired was close at hand. He started visualizing how Basileia would look in a few years, when he and Kratos would have their network of corruption well in place. "At last," he roared, "I will be their god!"

As Magos indulged himself in self-adoration, he didn't notice a streak of color emerging through the door. Matty had finally found a way into Magos' chamber. As he rounded the corner of the room, he pulled a small container of black adhesive from his vest that the team used back at the lab to fuse joints together on the simulator. He took the small, spongy blob out of its container and accelerated to full speed.

He had reached Kratos' evil attacker instantly and, in one swift motion, placed the adhesive directly over Magos' beaming implant. The beam released its hold on Kratos. Magos reached up to his implant to remove the sticky substance, only to find that it stuck to his hand as well as to his face. While he struggled, Matty streaked back to Kratos and shook him out of his temporary stupor. Within a few moments, Kratos refocused his thoughts and pulled a familiar item from inside his vest.

It was Teknon's Shocktech. Kratos had previously removed the Shocktech from his son's bag and allowed Arti to alter its design. Now the formerly feeble firearm was a fine-tuned instrument of precision. Kratos raised the Shocktech to eye level, aimed carefully, and fired. The narrow beam hit its target—the antenna on Magos' head. The fixture erupted with sparks as it flew from Magos, leaving the android with an open hole in his mechanized brain.

Magos stumbled around, still trying to remove the adhesive. Computer equipment began to explode in sequence around the room, and the video screens displayed a jumbled display of pictures and data. Kratos' theory had been correct: Magos controlled his entire empire through the antenna attached to his brain circuitry. With the antenna gone, so was the control Magos had over his equipment, including his android servants. Kratos and Matty noticed that the entire building seemed to be involved in a self-destruct sequence, with explosions igniting in every direction. Magos found himself surrounded in flames as the circuitry of the equipment throughout the room began to overload. He looked down at Kratos and yelled in a voice that was impaired by the chaos within and around him. "This is not over, Kratos," he shouted. "You *will* be mine one day!"

Kratos and Matty ran toward the door, hoping to get the others out before Sheol completely exploded.

"I leave you with one gift," Magos continued as the flames engulfed him. "I've lost all control of Sheol except for Dolios. He is programmed to survive even if I'm eliminated. He will succeed in destroying your beloved son."

Kratos tried to answer, but explosions threatened to seal off the exit from the chamber. "Let's find the others, quickly!" Kratos yelled.

*   *   *

"Dolios, I've heard a lot about you," Teknon managed to say.

"You idiot!" Dolios said, continuing his efforts to discourage Teknon. "How could I spend my life trying to create a man and end up with a loser like you? I should've gotten rid of you and your useless mother early on when I had the chance."

Teknon clenched his fists while the raging emotions of fear and anger tightened their grip on him. He didn't know whether to give in to his fears by running away, or to stay and battle the evil image of the man he loved and respected more than any other person. He closed his eyes for several seconds and spoke to someone unseen.

"Pneuma, please give me guidance. Clear my mind of fear and anger. Help me to see this evil machine as it really is so that I can complete my mission."

Teknon opened his eyes and faced Dolios. His fears were gone and his mind was at peace. Suddenly, something strange began to happen to his adversary. Dolios stood up straight, the evil expression vanishing from his face. His appearance began to change, too. Soon he changed to his true form, a small robot, almost the size of a toy. Teknon looked in amazement as Dolios turned and slowly shuffled into the darkness.

Teknon paused to make sure Dolios wasn't trying to trick him. Then he turned to the Logos and carefully placed his hands around it. Immediately, the sphere began to glow and illuminate the entire room. An image of a well-built man in uniform materialized a few meters away from Teknon. The man carried a shield displaying the emblem of the CHAMPION Warriors. The tall, rugged man looked at Teknon and began to speak. "Well done, warrior," the image said gruffly. "Now, prepare to fully learn the teachings of a CHAMPION!"

"Who are you?" Teknon said, in awe of the image.

"I am Didasko," the man replied. "And I will offer you principles of wisdom that will ignite your heart and give you the power to become a CHAMPION. As a CHAMPION, you will join us to change the galaxy for good."

The armored doors of the room flew open. Tor stood in the opening, his armbands smoldering. He looked around the room

and spotted Teknon, but Dolios was nowhere to be found. Matty streaked in and stood by Teknon's side. Teknon removed his hands from the Logos, and the image disappeared.

"Tek, are you all right?" Matty asked.

"Where is he?" Tor bellowed. "Where is this Dolios? I want to show him how a true CHAMPION can fight!"

"He's gone." Teknon replied. "I don't think we'll have any more trouble with him."

"You defeated him?" Epps asked, as he entered the room. Teknon nodded. "How?" Epps continued.

A cloud of rock and granitine appeared a few meters away. As soon as the swirling ceased, Phil chimed in. "I'll tell you how, Epps. Dolios was specifically created to conquer Magos' enemies by crippling them with fear. Teknon did not need to fight Dolios to defeat him. When Teknon allowed Pneuma to control his fear and chose not to respond to Dolios' attacks, Dolios' programming short-circuited. Well done, Teknon. Well done."

"And the Logos?" Arti asked. Teknon walked toward Arti and placed a circular object into his mentor's hands. Arti quickly placed the Logos in a special carrying case. The team gathered around to see the beauty and radiance of their prize. Kratos walked up, looked with relief at his son and the Logos, and then spoke to them. "There's no time to waste, my friends," he said firmly. "We must escape before this place gets blown off the planet."

The team members scrambled out of the room, through the halls, and out of the tower. On the way, they spotted numerous footsoldiers and kakos, frozen in position. The mindless androids were hopelessly disabled without the control and direction of their defeated master. Matty stayed in step with the rest of the team to help in any way he could. Phil burrowed beneath the group, checking for mines and ready at any time to create a bunker for his teammates that would shield them should the entire complex explode. They didn't stop running until they reached the summit of a nearby hill.

At the top of the hill, the CHAMPIONs turned around and watched the final explosive blasts, which toppled all the towers and momentarily turned the darkness into light. The team stood speechless, allowing their exhilaration of victory to engulf the moment. When the explosions finally subsided, they all hugged and shouted cries of celebration to each other and to their Warrior King.

The battle was finally over. The Logos was recovered. Mission accomplished.

EPISODE FIFTEEN

CELEBRATION

Close friends, relatives, and a few business associates roamed through the ballroom of the multilevel mansion suspended in the sky over Basileia. Paideia greeted every guest as they visited the numerous tables covered with elaborate dishes of food from around the world. She graciously thanked her guests for coming to honor the victory of her husband, her son, and the rest of their courageous team. They had defeated Magos and his evil creations on the planet Kairos. Now it was time to celebrate!

Teknon waited patiently on the observation deck of his father's expansive office suite. Kratos had arranged to meet him in the office before the formal celebration started. Teknon gazed over the snow-white clouds that floated above Basileia. He could see the ridges of Mount Purgos piercing through the mist like the fingers of a giant hand reaching through the ceiling. As he viewed the breathtaking beauty, his mind drifted back to the mountain trail on Kairos where he first committed his life to Pneuma and became united with Him.

The thought of an all-powerful, personal Spirit in control of his life gave everything new meaning. Basileia was not only a place to live, it was where his future mission would take place. Teknon glanced across the office to see the Logos sitting in its new, but temporary, perch. He knew that soon the Logos would be restored to its proper place on Basileia. Teknon now had a purpose in his life. He was thankful for his new relationship with the Warrior King and he was glad to be home.

The door to the office burst open, and a dark blur darted inside, screeching to a halt. Matty stood proudly, his hands on his hips, looking straight at Teknon. His eyes glanced up and down, closely examining Teknon's new uniform. The swift mentor's eyewear snapped back from his eyes, and he gave his young friend a cocky smile. "Well, Tek, how do you like the new threads?" Matty asked. "Just wanted you to know, I helped design 'em. I thought you could use an outfit with a little more style."

"Who cares about style?!" a voice bellowed from the hallway. "It's the uniform of a CHAMPION. Never forget it!"

"I won't, Tor," Teknon replied grinning. He watched as Epps, Arti, and Phil flooded into the office and gathered around him. But there was no sign of Kratos. "Where's Dad?" he said.

"He'll be here momentarily," Phil said, munching on the marinated stalk of a vealplant.

"Why does he want us to meet in here?" Teknon asked.

"I guess we'll find out soon enough," Epps said, pointing toward the door.

Kratos entered his office, also wearing a new uniform. Teknon watched proudly as his father walked across the room, his broad shoulders held back and his head high. The mentors parted as Kratos walked between them and stopped in front of Teknon.

Kratos looked into his son's eyes, then spoke as if he were making a formal speech to one of his classes at the institute. "Today, Teknon, we celebrate. We are joining together to recognize our team's first victory in a much larger war against evil. You were an important part of that victory. You faced your greatest fear in the process, and defeated it. You also learned to recover from your failures.

"Look at the men around you. They are part of your team. They are committed to you and to your future success. They have much to offer you. But they expect that you will continue to be a contributing member of their team, committed to their success and to the success of our mission. Is that your desire?"

Teknon gazed into the faces of his mentors. His eyes moistened as images of these men and their heroic efforts flashed through his memory. He cared deeply about them, and he appreciated their commitment to him. "It *is* my desire," Teknon said fervently. "It's *my* mission as well."

"Then I must ask you for something," Kratos continued, reaching his hand forward. "Give me your Hoplon."

Teknon's happy expression changed to one of confusion. "Why? Did I say something wrong?"

"No," Kratos responded. "I told you on Kairos that one day I might ask you to return your Hoplon to me. Do you remember?"

Teknon nodded slowly. "I remember. You want it now?"

"Yes," Kratos said.

Teknon walked over to his shield, which sat upright in its harness. Both Hoplons were stored in elaborate twin cases, ready for quick access in case of an emergency. Teknon pressed the release button on the case and reluctantly removed his shield. His hands affectionately felt their way across the CHAMPION Warrior emblem as he walked back to his father. He held out the shield with both hands. Kratos quickly took it and placed it underneath his arm.

"I'll see you in a few minutes," Kratos said, as he turned and marched deliberately out of the room.

"I don't get it," Teknon said sadly. "I thought Dad said I was ready for a Hoplon."

"Don't worry about it, Tek," Matty said abruptly. Then he turned to the others and grinned. "Well, I don't know about you guys, but I intend to get my share of the desserts before the ceremony starts. Care to join me?"

Several other mentors followed, but Teknon hung behind and looked out of the window again. Epps, watching Teknon, joined him at the window and looked out over the clouds and mountain ranges. He glanced at Teknon from the corner of his eye. "Magnificent view," the mentor said. "I hear it's the most expensive office space on the planet or above it for that matter."

Teknon produced a small grin. "Yeah, it's quite a place."

"You know," Epps said, "I've been meaning to ask you something. Why do you think Dolios appeared as your father? Why did the image of Kratos represent your greatest fear?"

Teknon thought for a few seconds before responding. He took a deep breath and sighed. "I wasn't scared of Dad," Teknon replied. "It was the image of him as an evil man, without purpose or morals, that shook me to my boots. I've always loved and admired my dad for his standards and example. I've never thought of him any other way. Seeing Dad's image like that was more frightening than anything I could imagine." Teknon paused. "Does that make sense, Epps?"

"Perfectly," Epps said. "And because you knew your dad trusts in and draws his strength from Pneuma, you knew he wouldn't allow himself to become like that evil image, and you determined not to allow that fear to overtake you."

"That's right," Teknon affirmed.

"Kratos is a man worthy of your trust and admiration and Pneuma is always faithful," Epps said, placing his hand on his young friend's shoulder. "Never doubt that for a moment. Now, why don't we join the others before Matty polishes off all of the goodies?"

Teknon nodded and followed Epps toward the ballroom. On the way, Teknon's younger sister, Hilly, passed him in the hall, her face turned slightly away to avoid eye contact with her brother.

"Hey, Hilly," Teknon said looking back at his sister, "nice outfit."

Hilly spun arown on her heels. "What?"

"I said, nice choice of clothes for the celebration. By the

way, Mom said you needed some help on your geometric equations."

"Yeah, so?" Hilly answered cautiously.

"How 'bout we take a look at them together. Say, maybe tomorrow night after dinner?"

"Well, yeah, sure," Hilly said, smiling. "That would be great. Thanks."

Teknon returned the smile and continued after Epps to the ballroom.

Teknon's eyes widened as he entered the room. The guests were standing in front of a raised platform. Kratos and the rest of the team stood on top of the platform, looking down at their youngest teammate. Teknon noted that the chancellor of Basileia, Admiral Ago, had also joined the team on the platform. Sweat beaded on Teknon's forehead as he noticed that the rest of the crowd also had their eyes fixed on him. Kratos stepped forward to the edge of the raised landing. He looked at his son, and spoke loudly without the aid of voice amplification. "Come forward, my son," he pronounced.

Teknon glanced curiously at his father, and then smiled to the guests as he walked past them and up to the top of the platform. Kratos motioned for him to stand in the middle of the stage. Teknon looked at his mentors with confusion as he responded to his father's direction.

"My friends," Kratos said, turning to the audience, "today we have much to celebrate. Pneuma granted us victory during our mission to Kairos. He guided us every step of the way and accomplished His purposes through us. Today we offer Him our thanks as well as our continued dedication.

"And due to the brave and heroic efforts of the men standing before you," Kratos continued, pointing the mentors and Phil, "we have won the first battle against the evil that threatens our precious homeland." A cheer erupted from the crowd as Kratos continued. "These men risked their lives to stop Magos and to return the only complete archive of Pneuma's teachings to our people. I am, of course, referring to the Logos.

"But I also want you to know that my son, Teknon, played

a vital role in the success of our mission. Because of his teachable attitude, his willingness to learn the principles of CHAMPION Warrior combat, and his eventual commitment to the Warrior King, he contributed a great deal to our endeavor.

"Today I want to make a public declaration to my friends and family. Because of my son's personal growth during our mission, and because of his desire to become a permanent member of our team, I want to acknowledge to you today that he is no longer a boy, but is indeed a fine young man, an individual worthy to be called a 'CHAMPION in Training.' He has started his journey toward real manhood, toward becoming a true CHAMPION Warrior."

As the crowd again erupted in applause, Kratos reached into a concealed compartment and produced Teknon's shield. Teknon's mouth dropped open as he looked at the beautiful weapon. It glistened in the ballroom lights. Kratos walked over to his son and held the shield out to him. As Teknon placed his hands on the Hoplon, Kratos again spoke.

"When I took this Hoplon from you, it was recognized only as Teknon's shield. Now, I give it back to you proudly, to be known forevermore as the "Shield of Pneuma," a tool to be used in His service. Use it, my son, to aid your team, to fulfill your mission, and to honor your Warrior King."

Teknon received the Hoplon firmly in both hands and fixed his eyes on Kratos. Then he handed his shield to Epps and embraced Kratos warmly. The rest of the team members crowded around the young man to offer words of encouragement and praise.

All at once, Tor and Arti raised Teknon into the air and walked him around the stage in a victory march, acknowledging their friend's transition into young manhood.

Admiral Ago raised his hands in the air to calm the applause. "Ladies and gentlemen," he bellowed in his deep and authoritative tone, "as we enter a new era of purpose for the people of Basileia, the time has come for us to revive an ancient fighting unit that our ancestors recognized as the flagship in their mission to battle evil and change their world for Pneuma's glory." Then he pointed to the team. "It is my privilege to present to you the New League of CHAMPION Warriors!"

Excitement and cheering filled the great ballroom. Many guests rushed up to the landing and congratulated the team. The warriors enjoyed numerous slaps on the backs from the men and hugs from the ladies as they retold the adventures of their journey.

Later, as Teknon finished sipping his drink, he noticed his father and Arti across the room talking in intense, hushed tones about something obviously important. Teknon watched curiously as Kratos motioned for Arti to go back into the office. Then Kratos walked back toward the ballroom with a firm expression on his face.

Kratos calmly gathered the attention of the other team-mates and gestured for them to join him in the office. Then he strode quickly to Teknon and whispered, "Come into the office. There's a problem."

Teknon put his glass down and followed his father through the large sliding door into the office—now the head-quarters for the New League of CHAMPION Warriors. The team members were focusing on the large, luminous table map in the center of the room. Teknon was surprised to see Admiral Ago also looking at the map, with one hand stroking his chin as if he were trying to solve a dilemma.

"Tell them the situation, Arti," Kratos said.

"Something caught my eye as I walked by the office a few minutes ago," Arti said, looking directly at Admiral Ago. "This map is directly linked to our observation satellite, which orbits Basileia. I programmed the satellite to alert us if there were any indications of fibronic emissions or tantronic energy on the planet. The map was blinking when I came in." Arti pointed to a light flashing on the map like a tiny beacon. "There it is." Silence filled the room as everyone gazed intently at the small flickering light on the three-dimensional image. A full minute went by before someone finally broke the silence.

"All right, men, let's move!" Tor said, grinning. "I'm ready to roll 'em." He reached for the vault that contained his arm braces. In two snaps, he was armed and ready for battle.

"Try to identify where he's located, Kratos," Admiral Ago said sternly. "We want to prevent the creation of another Sheol if at all possible."

Teknon looked around in amazement. "Sheol?" he said. "You mean Magos? I thought ... "

"Nah," Matty said, fastening the closing fixtures on his shoes. "We probably just nicked the brainy beast back on Kairos. Now the real fun begins."

"You mean he's here on Basileia?" Teknon asked. "We didn't get rid of him on Kairos? I don't believe this. It's starting all over again!"

"No, Son," Kratos said, as the other team members bustled around, getting their gear, "it's continuing. Our victory in Sheol was just the first battle. Magos is incredibly resourceful. We suspected that we wouldn't defeat him immediately. He's been creating his network on Kairos and Basileia for many years. And now, of course, we have an even bigger enemy to fight."

"You mean Poneros?" Tor grumbled. "We know so little about him other than he must be inherently evil and incredibly brilliant. It's hard to imagine that Magos would answer to anyone. Combined, they will be quite formidable."

"Yes, they will," Kratos replied, while packing his belt with energy bars. "But now we have a fully operational team to battle against their strategies. And, more importantly, we have the power of Pneuma to wage war against them."

"Whoa!" Teknon said, as he paused to think. "But what about the celebration? What about all that good food and fun we were supposed to have?"

Epps laughed at Teknon's response, as his gloves expanded and glistened in the light shining through the window. Arti carefully adjusted his face band and attached the Sensatron to his belt. Tor started walking toward the particle assimilator, and then stopped to yell to his young companion. "Well, kid," Tor barked, "I mean, young CHAMPION, are you coming or not?"

"You know the answer to that," Teknon said excitedly.

Teknon picked up his harness, then ran over to Epps and retrieved his Hoplon. He placed his shield behind his back, and felt the adrenaline rush through his body as it attached to its brace.

The other members of the team were already on the assimilator platform when Teknon arrived and took his position. Admiral Ago's face revealed his tension as he stood behind Phil, who was at the controls.

"Phil," Kratos said, looking at his friend, "Arti will contact you when it's time for you to join us. Keep an eye on the screen and alert us to any pertinent changes."

Phil nodded as he adjusted the controls, precisely targeting the coordinates. "I look forward to our rendezvous. May Pneuma protect and strengthen you."

"Battle well, my friends," the admiral said to his elite fighting unit. "May Pneuma give you courage and strength in your mission."

Kratos looked around at his team. All five of their faces fixed forward with a look of focused determination. Kratos smiled proudly to himself as he glanced at the young man standing at his side. Then he voiced the traditional creed.

"For His honor and glory!"

"For His honor and glory!" the others responded as they vanished from the assimilator platform.

The mission continued.

SERGIO CARIELLO '98

The CHAMPION Code

(Characteristics of a CHAMPION Warrior)

Character is the moral strength that grows out of our relationship with Pneuma*. Personal growth in character is expressed through the physical, emotional, social, mental, and especially spiritual areas of our lives.

Courage

I will cultivate bravery and trust in Pneuma. I will break out of my comfort zone by seeking to conquer my fears. I will learn to recover, recover, and recover again.

Honor

I will honor Pneuma by obeying Him and acknowledging Him as the complete source of my life, both now and through eternity. I will treat my parents, siblings, friends, and acquaintances with respect. I will appreciate the strengths and accept the weaknesses of all my "team members."

Attitude

I will cultivate a disposition of humility. I will assume a correct and hopeful view of myself as a member of Pneuma's family. I will improve my ability to manage anger and discouragement. I will develop and enjoy an appropriate sense of humor.

Mental Toughness

I will allow Pneuma to direct my thinking toward gaining common sense and wisdom. I will use discernment when making hard decisions. I will desire respect from others rather than compromise my convictions for acceptance or approval.

CHAMPION CODE

PURITY

I will train myself to keep the temple of my body and mind uncorrupted mentally, emotionally, and physically. I commit to avoid and flee sexual temptation.

INTEGRITY

I will seek to acquire a clear understanding of who I am in Pneuma so that I may have a deeper comprehension of what I believe, what I stand for, and how I can live out those convictions in the most difficult circumstances, whether I am alone or with others. I will allow other people to hold me accountable to standards of excellence.

OWNERSHIP

I will apply effective stewardship by using my life and the resources Pneuma entrusts to me—including my possessions, time, and talents—for His glory. I will seek contentment in Pneuma's provision for my needs. I will learn to practice delayed gratification.

NAVIGATION

I will allow Pneuma to chart my course by accepting my mission from Him, and I will complete that mission by trusting in Him. I will study the Logos, Pneuma's Word, so I can know Him better and gain His strength and direction for my life. I will become goal-oriented by learning to focus my attention on completing worthwhile short-term and long-term objectives.

* Note: The character Pneuma represents God in this fictional story.

Mentor Guide
(father's handbook)

Fiction novel

Mission Guide
(son's handbook)

FREE WALL POSTER OF THE
CHAMPION WARRIORS

Action-Packed
CHAMPION
Adventure Program

Who's training your son to become a man?

In this breakthrough adventure program for fathers and sons, FamilyLife has developed an easy-to-use format that will keep both you and your son excited about the mentoring process. You *can* develop a young man who can stand against negative peer pressure, make wise choices, and influence others positively.

◆ Develop a closer relationship with your son through fun, action-packed activities
◆ Explore courageous manhood and godly character in 16 interactive sessions
◆ Deepen your son's convictions as you discuss real-life issues and biblical truths
◆ Bridge the gap to manhood with a tailor-made manhood ceremony

… Adaptable for groups and single moms

To learn more or to order the Adventure Progam, visit www.familylife.com/teknon or call 1-800-FL-TODAY.

Start your son on his mission to manhood today!

GLOSSARY

Admiral Ago (ăd′mər-əl ä′go) – Chancellor of the planet Basileia and good friend to the CHAMPION movement

amacho (ə-mä′chō) – Fierce beast that roams Kairos, often hunting in packs. Large claws, powerful legs, and a poisonous barbed tail allow it to prey on other animals.

Ameleo (ä-mē′lē-o) – Overindulgent father of Pikros and Parakoe, who meets the CHAMPION Warriors on the *Ergonaut*

amuno (ə-mo͞o′nō) – Fighting style of the CHAMPION Warriors taught to Kratos and then to Teknon by Tor, Epps, Arti, and Matty. Primarily focused on defense, it resembles several martial arts disciplines.

android (ăn′droid) – Mechanical robotic creature

Apoplonao (ä-pŏp′lŏn-ā′ō) – Perasmian maiden, nicknamed Lana, whom Teknon meets at a spring-fed pool near Bia. Lana is actually Scandalon disguised as a beautiful young lady.

Artios (är′tē-ōs) – Nicknamed Arti, he is a mentor to Teknon and member of the CHAMPION movement. An amuno master from the Mache Region, Arti created a face band that enables him to shoot a paralyzing ray or a beam that identifies individuals or objects cloaked by a holographic image.

Basileia (băs-ĭ′lē-ə) – Home planet of Kratos, Teknon, the mentors, and Magos

Basileia Technology Institute (BTI) – Famous university on Basileia that produces many of the engineers and inventors for the planet. This is also the school where Kratos and Phil met.

Bia (bē′ə) – Small, rugged town on the planet Kairos where Kratos and Teknon meet the Harpax gang

bionic (bī-ŏn′ĭk) – Having physical characteristics enhanced by electrical or mechanical components

biosynthetic matrix (bī′ ō-sĭn-thət′ ĭk   mā′ trĭks) – Technology designed by Magos and Kratos that allows a human to merge his mind and body with computer circuitry. Magos further develops this technology to provide what he believed to be mechanized immortality.

CHAMPION (chăm′ pē-ən) – One who exhibits Courage, Honor, Attitude, Mental Toughness, Purity, Integrity, Ownership, and Navigation as he battles evil and changes his world for Pneuma's glory

cyborg (sī′ bôrg) – A being that is partly human and partly machine

Daimons (dā′ mənz) – An evil army of aggressors that threatened to overthrow Basileia in the days of the ancient League of CHAMPION Warriors

Didasko (dī-dăs′ kō) – One of the CHAMPION instructors who can be accessed through the Logos

digmite (dĭg′ mīt) – Small, carnivorous insect, capable of inflicting a painful, fever-inducing bite

dinar (dĭ-när′) – Basic currency used on the planet Basileia

domicat (dŏm′ ə-kăt) – Tame and calm domestic house pet

Dolios (dō′ lē-ōs) – An extremely powerful kako android created by Magos that guards the Logos. Dolios has the ability to appear in the form of his opponent's greatest fear.

Epios (ĕp′ ē-ōs) – Nicknamed Epps, he is a mentor to Teknon and a member of the CHAMPION movement. He comes from the Mache Region and is an amuno master. Epps created special gloves that allow him to heal injuries and illnesses, as well as cause the people he touches to become completely honest and friendly for a brief period of time.

Ergo (ûr′ gō) – Resort town on the planet Kairos, where Kratos, Teknon, and Matty battle the amachos

Ergonaut (ûr′ gō-nôt) – Cruise ship that shuttles between Ergo and Sarkinos on the planet Kairos

Eros (ĕr′ ōs) – Host of one of the holographic imaging salons in the Sarkinos Underground

fibronic (fī-brän´ ĭk) – Consisting of a special technology that enables digital transmissions between androids

footsoldier (fŏŏt´ sōl-jər) – Mindless android created by Magos primarily for the purpose of maintaining security for Sheol and destroying his enemies

florne (flôrn) – White, sweet-smelling, delicious, and soothing drink

gleukos (glōō´ kōs) – Intoxicating drink that produces a mind-altering effect similar to alcohol or marijuana

gorgon (gôr´ gŏn) – Dangerous reptilian creature that ranges from five to 10 meters in length

hammerhoop (hăm´ ər-hōōp´) – A popular Basileian sport where opposing teams of three players each attempt to send a spherical "pulsar" into statically energized nets called chambers, as they avoid being swatted by mechanized arms used to guard the chamber area. The game is played in an anti-gravity environment and requires tremendous physical conditioning.

Harpax (här´ păks) – Attractive but vicious race of people, who use their strength and intelligence to hurt, rather than help, others. Harpax usually travel in para-military gangs.

Hedon Bay (hē´dən bā) – Body of water on the planet Kairos that lies south of the Northron Peninsula and empties into the sea north of the Thumos Mountain range

Hilarotes (hĭ-lâr´ ə-tēz´) – Teknon's sister, nicknamed Hilly, and daughter of Kratos and Paideia

hodgebeast (hŏj´ bēst) – Large, aggressive mammal with long tusks that spike upward from its lower jaw. Its fur is short and coarse, and it emits a strong, unpleasant odor.

holographic image (hŏ-lə-grăf´ ĭk ĭm´ ĭj) – Artificial, three-dimensional (3D) representation of a real-life object or environment produced by sophisticated laser technology

holographic image salon – Establishment where people go to view and interact with sexually oriented holographic images for entertainment

Hoplon (hŏp´ lŏn) – The highly technical, multi-dimensional shield created by Kratos and Phileo

hoverboard (hŭv´ er–bôrd) – Aerodynamic piece of sporting equipment used on Basileia to ride snow-covered slopes or the crest of large waves on the coastline

Hudor Sea (hoo´ dôr sē) – Body of water on the planet Kairos that Teknon, Kratos, Matty, and Tor cross on the *Ergonaut*

hydronic engine (hī–drŏn´ ĭk ĕn´ jĭn) – Powerful machine that produces its own energy through an ingenious pro-tonic regenerating process developed by Kratos. Because if its capabilities, only three engines are required to main-tain the elevated status of the suspended mansion.

hydrovessel (hī´ drō–vĕs–əl) – Aquatic transport ship pro-pelled by engines that force water through the hull of the ship and out the back

infra-illuminator (ĭn´ frə–ĭ–loo´ mə-nā-tər) – Infrared light device that allows sub-light vision capabilities without revealing its location to surveillance systems

interactive non-woven alloy – Man-made fiber constructed by Matty to create his suit. The filament is interactive at a molecular level, performing when desired as a chemical catalyst in the body to produce great speed.

Kairos (kī´ ros) – Planet where Kratos, Teknon, and their team battle Magos and attempt to retrieve the Logos

kako (kā´ kō) – Type of powerful android created by Magos and programmed to carry out his instructions. Kakos have the ability to process information and make deci-sions. Several, such as Scandalon and Dolios, have spe-cial abilities.

keline (kē´ lĭn) – Domesticated animal on Kairos, which pro-vides delicious meat for consumption

kilometer (kĭl´ ə-mē´ tər) – Unit of measurement to determine longer distances on Basileia, equal to one thousand meters or 0.62 miles

Kopto (kŏp´ tō) – Commercial town where Kratos, Teknon, and the rest of their team first arrive on Kairos

Kopto Commercial Market – Large, outdoor shopping market located in the city of Kopto

Kratos (krā´ tōs) – Father of Teknon and leader of the new CHAMPION movement

Lacerlazer (lā´ sər-lā´ zər) – Powerful tool used by the Phaskos to penetrate the hard surface of Kairos for the purpose of mining

Lady Trophos (trō´ fōs) – Owner of the tavern in the Thumos Mountains and an undercover operative working against Magos

leviathan (lə-vī´ ə-thən) – Large, aggressive sea creature that hunts off the Northron coast and is a threat to swimmers

locator beacon – Small transmitting device that allows Paideia to track Kratos and his team via satellite, wherever they might be

Logos (lō´ gös) – Small, spherical object that holds all of the teachings of the CHAMPION Warriors

Maches (mä´ shāz) – Warriors from the Mache Region of Basileia, known as the only remaining tribe on the planet that practices amuno, the fighting style of the ancient CHAMPION Warriors

Mache Region (mä´ shā rē´ jən) – An isolated and rugged area of Basileia that is home to Tor, Epps, Arti, and Matty

Magos (mä´ gōs) – Old friend of Kratos, turned evil cyborg (part human, part android) and enemy to the CHAMPION movement. The fixture on the side of Magos' head enables him to control all of the creatures and computer equipment in his empire.

mamonas (mä-mō´ näs) – Valuable mineral used to produce memory chips for highly advanced computer equipment

Mataios (mä-tā′ ōs) – Nicknamed Matty, he is a mentor to Teknon. Matty comes from the Mache Region and is a member of the CHAMPION movement. Matty created a suit that enables him to attain incredible speed, protective eyewear that gives him 360-degree vision, and boots that allow him to easily scale walls and other vertical surfaces.

mentor (měn′ tôr) – One who helps, teaches, and cares for another person. Teknon's mentors are all committed to helping and training him to become a CHAMPION Warrior.

meter (mē′ tər) – Fundamental unit of measurement to determine length; equivalent to 3.28 feet

molecular matrix (mə-lěk′ yə-lər mā′ trĭks) – Cell level structure of a person or object that can be restructured and transmitted via particle assimilator to other locations

Mount Purgos (mount pûr′ gōs) – Magnificent mountain on the planet of Basileia, near the home of Kratos, Padeia, Teknon, and Hilly

nela (nē′ lə) – Soothing beverage that can be served either hot or cold, made from the ground leaves of the nela plant grown on Basileia

neurosynaptic (noo′ rō-sĭ-năp′ tĭk) – Pertaining to the process that occurs when transmissions are sent from the brain across the nervous system of the human body and into the devices developed by the various CHAMPION Warriors. For example, the Hoplon responds to Kratos' brain waves.

Northros (nôrth′ rōs) – Small, primitive town located on the Northron Peninsula of Kairos, and a temporary stopping place for the CHAMPION Warriors before they entered the Thumos Mountains

Paideia (pā-dē′ ə) – Wife of Kratos, mother to Teknon, and a member of the CHAMPION team

Parakoe (pâr′ ə-kō) and **Pikros** (pĭk′ rōs) – Immature teenage brothers and sons of Ameleo who meet Teknon on the *Ergonaut*

Paranomia (pâr-ə-nō´mē-ə) – Nicknamed Pary, she is the beautiful girl from Northros whom Teknon finds attractive and spends time with

particle assimilator – Common device designed to transport individuals and objects instantly from one place to another through transformation of their molecular matrix

Perasmos (pâr-ăs´mōs) – Thick forest on Kairos that Kratos and Teknon travel through on their way to Bia

phago (fä´gō) – Very large reptilian creature with long claws and fangs. It can grow to 25 meters in height and is a natural predator of the amachos.

Phasko (făs´kō) – Group of mining people located on Kairos. Short and powerful, they have the ability to drill through the ground with incredible speed and accuracy.

Phileo (fĭl-ā´ō) – Also called Phil, he is a Phasko and long-time friend to Kratos

Plutos Region – Tropical territory on the coast of the Hudor Sea where Kratos and Teknon enter the lavish resort of Ergo

Poroo (pō-roō´) – Distinguished but arrogant manager of the resort town of Ergo

Poneros (pə-nâr´əs) – Inherently sinister, powerful, and brilliant evil master of Magos

Pneuma (noō´mə) – The eternal Warrior King whom the CHAMPION Warriors follow and serve. He is the all-powerful Spirit who desires that all people choose to come into a personal relationship with Him.

Pseudes (soōds) – Informant for Magos in the Sarkinos Underground who reveals all he knows to the CHAMPION team after Epps touches him with his special gloves

Rhaima (rā´mə) – Small planet inhabited by prison colonies

Rhegma (rĕg´mə) – Leader of the Harpax gang whom Kratos and Teknon encounter in the town of Bia

sabercamel (sā´bər–kăm´ əl) – Tri-hump, foul-smelling, shaggy beast used primarily for transporting cargo across desert terrain

sandsnipe (sănd´snīp) – Small, foul-smelling Basileian rodent, which can produce a noxious liquid spray from its nose if provoked

Sarkinos Underground (sär´kə-nōs ŭn´dər–ground´) – Also know as Lower Sarkinos, a popular adult entertainment community on Kairos that offers gambling, luxurious lodging, holographic imaging salons and other forms of illicit entertainment

Scandalon (skăn´dl-ŏn) – Kako android and one of Magos' most dangerous creations. Scandalon has the ability to change his appearance to whatever form will cause the most harm to Kratos, Teknon, or whomever else he targets as an enemy. He works primarily through the methods of deception and seduction.

scratchbacks (scrăch´băks) – Thieves and murderers who form nomadic gangs of that roam the dark alleys in urban areas on the planet Basileia

seismos (sīz´mōs) – Large, thick-skinned carnivore that roams the Thumos Mountains

Sensatron (sĕn´sĭ-trŏn) – Small diagnostic device that Arti carries on his belt. The Sensatron can take many different kinds of readings, including weather, enemy advancement, and material composition.

sheepalopes (shēp´ ə-lōps) – Mindless domestic animals that are used for food and clothing

Sheol (shē´ōl) – Fortress and headquarters of Magos located deep in the Thumos Mountains. Sheol can be readily recognized by its three large, sinister towers.

Shocktech (shŏk´tĕk) – Hand-held weapon purchased by Teknon at the Kopto Commercial Market

speca (spĕ´kə) – Basic unit of currency used in the Kopto Commercial Market on the planet of Kairos

spike rat (spīk′ răt) – Small, barely edible rodent found along the trails of Kairos

swampcrusher (swŏmp′ krŭsh-r) – Carnivorous, multi-tentacled creature that lurks in the rivers of the Basileian rain forests

tantronic energy (tăn-trŏn′ ĭk ĕn′ ər-jē) – Highly volatile and dangerous power source that can vaporize human flesh if the energy intensity is high enough

Tarasso (tär-ăs′ ō) – Region on planet Karios west of the Hudor Sea where the city of Sarkinos is located

Teknon (tĕk′ nŏn) – Son of Kratos and Paideia and primary character in the story

ten high – Card game usually associated with gambling and played frequently in the Sarkinos Underground casinos

Tharreo (thär-rā′ ō) – Nicknamed Tor, this mentor to Teknon is from the Mache Region. He is second in command on the CHAMPION Warrior team and an amuno master. Tor created arm braces that enable him to fire energy beams that can lift and hold tremendous weight. The beams increase Tor's already enormous strength.

Thumos Mountains (thōō′ mōs) – Treacherous mountain range on Kairos known for violent weather changes and dangerous terrain

transfer station – Place where travelers can start and end trips using a particle assimilator

transtron racer (trăns′ trŏn) – Sleek, fast vehicle that can hover several meters above the ground

transparent carbonic alloy – Clear, impenetrable man-made substance constructed in a patented process that uses several rare elements found on both Basileia and Kairos

vealplant (vēl′ plănt) – Delicious vegetable that is large enough to be cut into servings that resemble steaks

wartmouse (wôrt′ mous) – Small, sharp-toothed rodent capable of eating five times its body weight each day

Acknowledgments

Putting together an integrated program with a fiction novel for teens, an interactive training guide, and a comprehensive how-to manual for dads has been quite a challenge. There are a number of people I wish to thank for helping me to make *Teknon and the CHAMPION Warriors* a reality.

I would like to thank Neal and Ida Jean Sapp, Sam Bartlett, Sheri and Jack McGill, Dr. Gilbert Chandler, Martin Shipman, Don Jacobs, Roger Berry, Nick and Amy Repak, Michael Hohmann, Steve Bruton, Sergio Cariello, Rick Blanchette, Donald Joy, and Stephen Sorenson for their invaluable input and encouragement.

I also appreciate the dedicated team at FamilyLife for the theological, editorial, and design direction. This team includes Jerry McCall, Blair Wright, David Sims, Bob Anderson, Anne Wooten, and Fran Taylor.

My heartfelt thanks are extended to Ben Colter who, through his hard work and creative editing expertise, has helped to transform this material into an adventurous, user-friendly training program that we hope will greatly benefit both you and your son.

I want to thank my wife, Ellen, for striving with me to raise our children with strong character and for enduring the process of developing these materials. Last, but not least, I want to acknowledge my children, Katie, Kimberly, Kyle, and especially Casey for giving me encouragement and inspiration during the creative development of the CHAMPION Training adventure program. Thanks, kids!

About the Author

Brent Sapp is a first-time writer from Orlando, Florida. When his oldest son, Casey, was nearing the teen years, Brent developed a strong desire to intentionally prepare Casey for manhood. This desire produced many creative mentoring approaches and several key character principles. Brent has adapted these key CHAMPION principles into a futuristic adventure novel for preteen and teen boys. He has also developed an interactive character-building program for fathers to use with their sons as a companion resource to the novel (see page 212).

Brent and his wife, Ellen, have four children: Casey, Katie, Kimberly, and Kyle. Brent is a graduate of Florida State University, and has an MBA from Rollins College. He has worked in sales and marketing for the past 18 years. Brent and Ellen helped to bring the FamilyLife Marriage Conference to Orlando. They have also led a pre-marriage ministry at Northland Community Church.

About the Illustrator

Sergio Cariello is the talented free-lance illustrator behind the characters of *Teknon and the CHAMPION Warriors*. He also draws such well-known icons as Superman and Batman for DC Comics. In addition, he teaches at the prestigious Joe Kubert School of Cartooning and Animation. Sergio lives in South River, N.J., with his wife, Luzia.